Monster
of Farallon Islands

Lane Walker

The Fishing Chronicles
www.lanewalkerbooks.com

Monster of Farallon Islands by Lane Walker
Copyright © 2020 Lane Walker

ISBN 978-1-955657-07-5
For Worldwide Distribution
Printed in the U.S.A.

Published by Bakken Books
2021
www.lanewalkerbooks.com

To my son Rece, my favorite fishing buddy—
I hope you dream big and know
what a gift you are to all of us.

Hometown Hunters

The Legend of the Ghost Buck
The Hunt for Scarface
Terror on Deadwood Lake
The Boss on Redemption Road
The Day It Rained Ducks
The Lost Deer Camp

The Fishing Chronicles

Monster of Farallon Islands
The River King
The Ice Queen
The Bass Factory
The Search for Big Lou

For more books, check out:
www.lanewalkerbooks.com

-1-

The first time I saw her is a moment that will stay with me forever. The emotions I felt are hard to put into words. Fear ran cold through my body when the gigantic gray shark floated under our boat. She was too big to be real.

As the shark began to surface, her scars and war wounds began to materialize, hinting at her mysterious past. My initial fear turned to astonishment when I realized that this was probably one of the biggest sharks ever seen in the Pacific Ocean!

Was I cursed or the luckiest person on earth? Shaken and numb, I knew that this trip to the Farallon Islands would be one that I would never forget.

This stretch of the Pacific Ocean along the

California coast is different from the rest. It starts around Bodega Bay and extends south down the coast, stopping 50 miles past San Francisco in the Big Sur region. This area is known by the gruesome name of Red Triangle, due to the high number of shark attacks on humans, mostly caused by great whites. Last year in school we were shocked to learn that an estimated 38 percent of all great white shark attacks in the United States happen right there. Not too safe a place to be!

Growing up in the coastal town of Half Moon Bay put me smack dab in the middle of the Red Triangle. I often fished at the Farallon Islands, which is at the tip of the Red Triangle. The islands lie just 35 miles off our coast, and every fall they are invaded with gigantic white sharks.

I had no idea my love for fishing and the Pacific Ocean would bring me face to face with one of the biggest sharks ever recorded. I wasn't prepared for the monstrous shark or the dangerous adventure that followed.

My life was about to change forever.

-2-

The light-blue waves of the Pacific Ocean rocked our boat, *Orca II*, when we left Half Moon Bay Harbor that day. We steered clear of the dangerous waters north of Half Moon Bay where the waves could top off at over 60 feet. Today we were heading northwest towards the Farallon Islands.

Traveling to the islands wasn't exactly a pleasure cruise. The trip has a laundry list of challenges, especially in late October. Temperatures are in the low 50s in the mornings, making it a cold trip. The most difficult challenge is the high winds that blow this time of year. These high winds wreak havoc on the Pacific, causing waves of up to eight feet and making the ride in the *Orca II* feel like you're in a washing machine spin cycle. When you add in the heavy stream of sea spray and dense fog, going to the Farallon Islands can be downright treacherous. Sorry to say, the boat's small covered cabin offered little relief from the ocean's elements, plus it hampered the view.

Even with all the challenges, I never turned down a chance to fish with my dad on the charter boat. Inland fishing was fun, but there isn't a better feeling on earth than hooking into a giant halibut or striper out on the ocean. Today was a special day; it was Halloween. Dad and I were fishing for lingcod. One Saturday every month, Dad didn't book clients for fishing charters so he and I could fish together. It was my favorite day and one that he looked forward to as well.

The motor on the *Orca II* roared as we cut through the wind and the waves, heading due east straight to the Farallon Islands. The trip took around two to three hours, depending on the wind and waves. The loud, drawn-out humming sound of the boat and backdrop always hypnotized me. The Pacific Ocean offered a variety of colors and scenery that made me lose track of time.

I hardly noticed when the roar of the motor slowed to a dull hum. We had hit a large patch of dense fog, momentarily blocking our view of the ocean. Fog was a sure sign that we were finally close to the Farallon Islands. Most mornings during the fall, fog could be seen creating a thick wrap around the islands, helping to blanket its mysterious allure. Many ships were lost when they dared to venture too close to the misty Farallon Islands.

A strange rock formation magically appeared out of thin air, peaking through the heavy fog and signalling to us that we had arrived at our destination. The boat shook and swayed as Dad began to lower the anchor. Dad spent almost every day fishing the rich waters of the Pacific Ocean— both as a passion and a business. He always knew the best places to fish, especially near Farallon Islands.

I had most of the fishing poles baited and ready when Dad stepped out of the boat's cabin. The fishfinder had marked several large schools of fish, and we were hoping to hook into big lingcod, between 40-50 inches in size.

In a matter of minutes, I saw one of the tips of

the fishing poles bend into a familiar arched shape. The bite looked strong as I jogged over and jerked the rod to set the hook. We were bottom fishing in about 100 feet of water, so my pull was delayed a couple of seconds before I could feel the weight of the fish. I could tell instantly the fish was a good one, and it took a lot of strength to start reeling it up from the dark depths of the Pacific Ocean.

I reeled and reeled, straining with all the power a skinny 14 year old has. After the first few minutes, I slowed and gave my back and arms a quick rest to prepare for the rest of the battle.

The fish was tiring and getting closer to the top of the water. I felt the line relax, forcing me to intensify the strain on the line. Suddenly the pressure from the fish disappeared, and the line went completely limp.

Typically, a lingcod couldn't break our 40-lb braided fishing line. *Had I given it too much slack and allowed the fish to come unhooked?*

Disappointed with myself, I peered over the edge of the boat. I squinted, trying to see the light beige and pink belly of the lingcod through the murky water. I grabbed the edge of the *Orca II* and leaned over to get a better line of sight.

It was hard to see through the water since there seemed to be a shadow blocking my view. At first, I thought it was a large cluster of seaweed or maybe a shadow from the sun. Then it moved…

I squatted down on the deck of the boat to get a closer look. The gigantic shadow continued to move lazily, swimming under our boat. Suddenly I realized that it wasn't seaweed or a shadow; it was the dark outline of a great white shark!

Surprised, I jumped back and watched in amazement as an 18-foot great white passed under our boat, thrashing what was left of a lingcod in its monstrous jaws.

-3-

Native Americans used to call the Farallon Islands the "islands of the dead" because of their dangers. They also believed the islands were home to the spirits of their dead ancestors.

Mariners referenced the islands as "the devil's teeth" because of the number of shipwrecks associated with their treacherous coast. On a clear day, the islands' sharp, jagged cliffs are visible from the coastal beaches many locals call paradise.

Great white sharks migrate to the islands during the fall months and usually remain to feed there through late winter. The giant sharks fill the water and add to the diverse Farallon Island ecosystem.

The *Carcharodon Carcharias*, which is more

commonly known as the great white shark, is one of the most mysterious and intriguing animals. Over 450 shark species roam the world, but none rival the size or predatory skills of the great white. Adult great white sharks can grow up to 20 feet long, weigh over 6,000 pounds, and live for an estimated 30 years. Typically, females are much bigger than males.

Great white sharks are the perfect predators. Their jaws contain serrated blade-like teeth that can grow to over six inches in height, with the upper jaw having between twenty to thirty teeth. They can also swim up to 35 miles per hour, placing them at the top of the food chain.

Cool water and an abundant population of prey help make the Farallon Islands an ideal hunting grounds for white sharks. These sharks aren't the only gigantic animals roaming the Pacific Ocean, however. They share the water with huge blue and humpback whales and their only known enemy, killer whales.

To some, the Farallon Islands are the ultimate destination to view oceanic wildlife, a bucket list trip for whale watchers and shark enthusiasts alike. With all the names given to the Farallon Islands, I chose to call it something else, something much more personal. For me, the Farallon Islands were paradise. I fished the islands for the first time six years ago, and my stomach still churns with the same excitement and anxious butterflies.

The sights and smell of the islands are welcoming and familiar to me. Although the stench of the Farallon Islands was well known, it didn't bother me. The legendary odor of the islands can be smelled from ships a half mile away. The ammonia in bird and marine mammal feces casts a terrible smell.

I thought I knew a lot about the animals that called the Farallon Islands home and had studied most of them. Over the years, I had seen a lot of great white sharks on our trips fishing near the islands, but nothing like what I was about to encounter. I had no idea about the true dangers lurking in the turbulent waters off the islands of the dead.

-4-

Being raised near the golden sandy beaches in Southern California was a gift that I enjoyed every day. My life was pretty simple. Mom was a registered nurse at Seton Coastside Hospital in nearby Moss Beach. My 12-year-old sister, Sara, loved needles and blood and wanted to be a nurse like Mom. Me, I wanted to be just like my dad!

My dad owned a fishing charter business called Ultimate Saltwater Adventures that specialized in all kinds of saltwater fishing. The *Orca II* was a 38-foot Canaveral express cruiser decked out for fishing the great Pacific Ocean.

Our family has a unique love for the ocean. My mom had grown up in San Francisco and loved living near the beaches of Southern California. After she graduated from high school, she packed her bags for Milton, Massachusetts. She had accepted a full-ride athletic scholarship to play softball at a small Division III school called Curry College.

She had always dreamt of exploring the Atlantic Ocean and spending time near Cape Cod and Martha's Vineyard, so she sent Curry a highlight video of her playing softball. Once they saw the velocity on her fastball and the way the ball shook and dipped on her change-up, they offered her a scholarship.

Massachusetts was thousands of miles away from San Francisco. My Great-Aunt Joanie lived near Curry College in a town called Quincy. My aunt and the thought of a free college education was enough reason for her parents to let their baby girl leave the Golden State.

One weekend while sightseeing at Martha's Vineyard, she saw a crazy sun-bleached 20-year-old blond guy doing back flips off the American Legion Memorial Bridge. For some reason, my mom was smitten. Turns out that lunatic would later become my dad! He had spent his entire life in Martha's Vineyard, and when he wasn't fishing or scuba diving, he was working as a deckhand on a crab boat. They hit it off instantly and shared a strong, mutual passion for the ocean.

Dad's oceanic passion started at the age of seven when a director named Steven Spielberg invaded Dad's hometown of Famouth, just outside of Martha's Vineyard and began to film *Jaws*. One cool thing about the movie for our family was Dad being filmed as an extra in one of the beach scenes at the beginning. Our family has probably watched the movie over twenty times with Dad pointing out each time the three seconds where he and my grandma can be seen on the beach.

For my dad, watching *Jaws* being filmed started a journey of exploration and respect for the ocean and sharks. Not everyone saw sharks as my dad did. Shortly after the movie was released, a shark hysteria took over with the senseless killing of record numbers of sharks. It has taken conservationists and biologists several decades to change the man-eater narrative of *Jaws*.

Throughout high school, Dad fished and explored the coastal waters, enjoying his daily interactions with striped bass, white marlin, tuna, and a wide variety of sharks. Dad loved the Atlantic Ocean but always had a deep-rooted curiosity to explore the secrets of the Pacific.

Mom and Dad dated that entire year, and the next summer Dad flew out to Old Moon Bay to visit my mom and her family. That was all it took. After a weekend of fishing and diving in the rich Southern California waters with her, Dad was in love. The next week he got down on one knee and proposed to my mom at Pillar Point Harbor as the massive waves pounded the nearby rocks. Nine months later, the two were married and moved into a small two-bedroom house overlooking the Pacific shoreline of Half Moon Bay.

Mom never returned to Massachusetts but instead got her R.N. degree from a college in San Francisco, and Dad bought a charter fishing boat. He named it the *Orca II* in honor of the boat the sheriff and Quint used in *Jaws* to chase the giant great white shark.

That was the start of Ultimate Saltwater Adventures and our family. I was born first, then two years later my sister, Sara, came along, making us the James' family of four.

Maybe it was genetics, but from the first day I could remember, I loved everything about the ocean. My earliest memory was exploring the sandy local beaches. I remember when I was five years old and finding my first shark tooth. I thought I had found pure gold! Looking for shark teeth became a hobby, and I have collected hundreds in all shapes and sizes over the years.

It was hard to pinpoint what really attracted me to the ocean the most, but the blue waters, bright sunshine, and incredible pounding surf could make anyone fall in love with the California coast.

-5-

"Dad! Dad! Get over here!" I managed to yell in a high squeaky voice after I had seen that huge creature slide under our boat. Dad was standing at the front of the boat and threw down his rod and reel. He sprinted to the edge of the boat just in time to catch a glimpse of the giant back fin called the caudal fin of the great white.

"Careful, Casey, whites aren't the kind of fish you want to pet," Dad said with a chuckle.

Fishing the islands for the past twenty years had spoiled my dad when it came to great white sightings. Around town, Dad was known as a bit of a shark expert.

Great white sharks were my favorite animals on

the planet. It was a unique love affair filled with admiration and fear. Seeing a great white shark in person gave me a feeling of excitement but also made the hair on the back of my neck stand up. It was the perfect mix of excitement and fear that I felt every time I saw a white shark.

Even though I was only 14 years old, I had seen my share of great white sharks. This was definitely the biggest one I had ever seen.

"She's at least 18 feet, maybe more," Dad told me.

I assumed that the shark was a female since females are typically four to six feet longer than males. A male white shark averages between 11 to 14 feet, where females can be much bigger. We both rushed to the other side of the boat just in time to see the huge shark float by, bumping the *Orca II* with its top dorsal fin. The shark turned and disappeared back into the dark-blue waters surrounding the Farallon Islands.

What a rush! Seeing such a huge great white shark was awesome. We didn't let the shark keep us from fishing since we knew that at this time of year, the water around Farallon was always infested with huge sharks. We spent the next couple of hours bottom fishing, catching lingcod, rock cod, and one real nice striper. The striper put up a great fight and tested my angling skills. It was a great battle!

Sometime around mid-morning, the wind picked up. I glanced at our flag on the bow of the boat as it whipped violently back and forth. Dad was seasoned on the water, but high winds are something not even the most skilled mariner liked to deal with.

"We better get heading back to Old Moon," Dad said. I could tell by the way he was pulling up the lines that he was concerned with the shift in the wind. We pulled up the rest of the lines, but Dad noticed the last pole felt heavy.

"Son, reel this in quickly! I think there's something on it."

Dad handed me the pole and went into the cabin to start the engine. I reeled the rest of the line in before seeing a big rock cod on the end. Rock cod have a gorgeous orange color and are excellent to eat, so it was a good way to end our fishing trip.

"Casey, get that fish in, we need to jet," Dad yelled

in a concerned voice. I looked up towards the stern and could see the flag blowing even harder, but this time towards the crooked, jagged Farallon shores. I rushed into the cabin just as Dad hammered the boat's accelerator.

A storm was coming, and all the controls of our boat were loudly beeping and squawking. The front of the *Orca II* was cutting through the waves that continued to grow and pound the boat. The storm front shifted and was moving directly towards the islands. The rain started to pick up, masking them off from our view. Off to the horizon, the skies were dark-blue and gray. The waves were growing bigger and bigger; the only thing I could see was the crest of each one and then felt it crash. The storm had snuck up on us, but we weren't the only ones unprepared.

The loud thumping sound of the boat hitting the waves was replaced by a high-pitched buzzing sound coming from the *Orca II's* radio.

The buzzing suddenly stopped, and a man's muffled voice came on the radio with a strong Spanish accent that was hard for us to understand.

———

Dad reached down and adjusted some of the dials on the radio to make the audio clearer.

"Mayday! Mayday! Need immediate help! Large freighter *S.S. Atlantis* is taking on water. We're going down! Mayday! Mayday! I repeat!"

Dad quickly responded, "*Atlantis*, what is your location?"

"37°37′N 123°17′W. The ship is very heavy and sinking fast," cried the man.

"We are in route, not far, hold tight!" Dad quickly shouted.

He turned to me. "Get ready to help, Casey."

———

-6-

Dad entered the coordinates into our boat's GPS system. It was hard to see with all the waves crashing and the rain pouring down. We were close to the exact coordinates but still could see no sign of a boat.

As Dad crested the next wave, we caught sight of the sinking cargo ship in the distance. I had never seen a ship sink—it was frightening! The entire stern of the ship was completely under the water and going down rapidly with each wave. A black-and-green shadow in the water surrounded the boat and told us the gas and oil were leaking out and polluting the water.

As the *Orca II* pulled closer to the wreck, a

smaller lifeboat materialized. We pulled up and Dad threw a thick, heavy-duty braided rope across to the frightened crew. Four men wearing bright-orange life jackets were huddling in the lifeboat. The men were shouting in Spanish, but I couldn't make out what they were saying.

Dad and I pulled hard on the towline as the wind pounded the little boat. The lifeboat was taking on water, and we had to get the men safely aboard our boat as fast as possible. Nearby, smoke rose from the *Atlantis*, and the next wave that crashed onto the hull sank the entire vessel. The huge ship was gone.

The wind seemed to slow just long enough to pull the lifeboat to the *Orca II* and help the four crewmen climb on board. The drenched men crowded into our cabin, and I handed them some spare blankets.

"What happened?" Dad asked.

The men looked around at each other; it was obvious that they struggled to understand what Dad was saying.

One of the men from the back stepped forward. I was sure he was the captain of the ship.

"We are a shipping vessel out of Rosarito, Mexico," the captain explained in a thick accent. "We haul heavy granite rocks to a marina in Oak Harbor, Oregon." He had a seasoned look, so it was obvious this wasn't his first trip on the Pacific Ocean.

After wrapping the blanket around himself, he went on, "Everything was normal, just a typical trip, when our sonar picked up something in front of us. The objects were moving fast and in our direction. I didn't have time to turn. We saw several of the objects pass harmlessly under the boat; they were all pretty big. Then there was a loud boom and then another strange, crashing noise. The whole boat shook and rocked. Whatever it was, it ran directly into our large rear propeller."

I looked at Dad, and he had a puzzled look on his face. Running into something shouldn't sink a cargo ship the size of the *Atlantis*. *What could have possibly caused this ship to sink?*

Dad slowed the engine to a stop, idling in the churning water, and pointed out the back window of the boat.

"There's the answer to your mystery."

In the water between our boat and the *Atlantis* was the carcass of a freshly killed blue whale. The whale was almost completely cut in half. Blood and chunks of whale blubber and guts created a mushroom cloud around the animal's body. Even though the whale had been chopped in two and in rough shape, it was still enormous.

"I bet that whale is almost 90 feet long, probably weighs close to 150 tons. It looks like you had a pod of blue whales swim under your boat, and sadly, one hit the propeller," he said, shaking his head.

The overall scene was like something seen in a horror movie. It was strangely eerie considering today was Halloween. The water around the whale was bloody red and spreading fast. The mess was spreading through the blue Pacific waters.

Dad took the *Orca II* closer to examine the carcass. I had never been so close to a giant whale; we were close enough to touch it. Just as I reached down, I felt someone grab my arm. I turned to see one of the Spanish crew members pointing into the water.

Two large dorsal fins poked through the blood-red water and were circling the whale. The bodies slowly materialized, revealing two juvenile great white sharks, probably eight to nine feet in length. They didn't circle for long, as each shark darted into the whale to feed on it. The sharks were in an aggressive, frenzied state. They ripped and tore at the huge whale, although hardly making a dent in the beast's massive side.

Suddenly the sharks stopped, abandoning the fresh meat, and disappeared back into the depths of the ocean. I stood watching, wondering why any shark would give up such a tantalizing free meal. I headed back towards the cabin when I heard the Spanish captain yell.

"Mira, mira!" the Spanish captain shouted, pointing back at the whale carcass.

I turned to see the entire carcass shake, go under the water, and quickly pop back up. *What had the strength to pull the huge whale carcass underwater?*

Again the whale was floating alone, motionless in the ocean cur rent, but not for long. Seconds later a forceful shake once again jarred the carcass.

Another white shark was feeding on the whale, only this one was much bigger. A giant shadow materialized next to the whale, circling it. Suddenly a huge dorsal fin appeared with two distinct indentions.

The shark momentarily disappeared before shooting up vertically like a torpedo thrusting its giant jaws into the mid-section of the blue whale. The white shark hit with such speed and power, it rocked the entire whale carcass.

This shark was much bigger than the first two, probably pushing 20 feet in length. Even though the shark breached for only a few seconds, its unique size and top dorsal fin stood out.

"El Monstruo!" the captain quivered in an eerie voice.

While I wasn't fluid in Spanish, I had a good idea of what he said.

The Monster!

- 7 -

The rest of the trip back to Half Moon Bay was long and awkward. Our wet passengers were still in shock from their ship's sinking and the sighting of "Monster." I found it ironic that when I heard the word "monster," I thought of werewolves or Dracula—something evil and spooky. The shark was magnificent and glorious—a far cry from being a monster.

Eventually I made out the outline of Half Moon Bay Marina in the distance. As we drew closer, I starting seeing people milling around everywhere on the dock. It was obvious that news of our sea rescue had spread, and all the local mariners were anxious to see what had happened to the *Atlantis*. Dad threw the line to Jeff Fisher, captain of the boat

My Maria. Dad and Jeff had been friends for over twenty years, often fishing together around Half Moon Bay.

The crowd of people started to encircle us as we made our way down the dock. Everyone began asking questions about the ship. Two men in black suits headed straight through the onlookers towards the four crewmen. They walked them into the weigh station building and away from the crowd.

I felt the pressure of someone grabbing my arm. I turned and saw an old, familiar frail hand. Dad saw it too and glanced over his shoulder, realizing it was just Bones.

Bones was well-known and famous on the docks of Half Moon Bay. No one knew how old Bones was, but he was old! If I had to guess, I would say he was in his late 80s. Even though he was old, he was in great shape and was highly respected around town. His fishing and World War II stories were as legendary as his washed-out blue Navy *U.S.S. Independence* hat he always wore.

"Casey, what happened?" he asked in a low tone. I started to tell him everything, from the distress call to watching the big cargo ship sinking. When I got to the part of the whale carcass and the huge white shark, Bones became even more concerned.

"Where did that ship sink?" Bones demanded.

"I'm not sure, but Dad knows. I do know it was directly southeast of the South Farallon Island. We were fishing near Seal Rock," I said.

"How far south?" Bones quickly asked.

His questioning caught me off guard, so I had to step back and think. The waves, wind, and adrenaline we had experienced added to my confusion.

"We could still make out some of the island when the Mayday call came in. I'd guess we were somewhere between four to twelve miles from the South Island. The crew gave us the coordinates, the only number I remember from the distress call was 37, and I think it was used twice," I told him.

Out on the ocean, mariners commonly use latitude and longitude numbers for fishing and identification of locations when communicating with each other or mapping hot spots for fishing. For example, if we hit a hot spot and start catching a lot of fish, we mark the location on our onboard electronics. Then we can save the exact spot and go to it the next time we're out fishing.

Bones' body language shifted when I told him our location. He went from someone who seemed concerned to someone who was definitely afraid.

I looked around to make sure Dad was still close. He was being interviewed by a local television reporter from WPIX Channel 6. I listened to him talk about the ship, but he made no mention of the giant shark.

When I turned back to Bones, he was gone. Looking through the crowd, I couldn't see him anywhere. The whole encounter with Bones was strange and just added to the chaos and mystery of the day.

After the interview, Dad and I walked back to the parking lot and climbed into our truck.

"Dad, why didn't you mention the shark to the news reporter?" I asked.

Dad turned, "That shark is an alpha predator, top of the food chain. She shouldn't ever have to worry about becoming the prey."

-8-

"What did Bones want?" Dad asked as we got into the truck.

"I don't really know. It was weird. He wanted to know exactly where the ship sank," I said. "Who were the guys in the suits talking to the crewmen?"

"They looked like harbor masters. It turns out, our new Spanish friend's boat was way over the legal limit they were allowed to carry. The boat sank so fast because it was way too heavy for the Pacific," Dad explained.

That would also explain why the crew seemed so nervous about the sinking. Often large shipping companies try to cram as much cargo as they can onto boats and sneak them through the Pacific to make a higher profit. While it's illegal, it's hard to catch, so Dad wasn't surprised that the ship was overloaded.

"That ship was loaded with so much granite," Dad said, "it probably crashed straight to the ocean floor. I wouldn't be surprised if the noise served as a perfect dinner bell for all those great white sharks."

The blue whale carcass had filled the water with blood too, attracting all kinds of animals.

Dad quickly changed the subject. "I wonder what was up with Bones. That's weird. There isn't much that old bird hasn't seen."

Dad explained that Bones had served in the United States Navy as a nautical engineer. After serving ten years, he returned back to Half Moon Bay to work for some energy company out of San Francisco.

When we arrived home, Mom and Sara ran out to the truck.

"We were so worried about you two!" Mom cried out.

"I wasn't that worried about Casey—just Dad mostly," Sara said sarcastically.

Dad and I just laughed and went into the house to tell them about our amazing day while Mom prepared the fish that we had caught on our trip. She prepared pan-seared, lemon-crusted lingcod, and it was fantastic! Our family ate fish about four days a week, and Dad's charter fishing trip supplied most of it. Eating fresh, saltwater fish the day you catch them is the way to go.

The girls enjoyed our story about the day's daring adventure to Farallon Islands. When I told them the part about Bones questioning us on the docks, Mom found it strange as well but not Sara.

Sara quickly added, "That's not really strange for Bones. He's a creepy old guy who loves to tell tall tales and stories about his time in the Navy."

That night in bed I couldn't shake the image of the giant white shark torpedoing towards the dead blue whale. As magnificent as it was, it got me thinking about *El Monstruo* or "Monster" as the Spanish captain referred to it.

Two things I knew before falling asleep that night—the first was how misinformed people are about great white sharks. Monster was hardly ghastly or gruesome; she was gorgeous, a marvelous specimen of the Pacific. The second thing I knew was Bones knew something about the crash site that really bothered him.

A lot of ships sink in the vast depths of the Pacific Ocean, why was this one so important? Thankfully, I wouldn't have to wait long to get my answer.

-9-

Sunday is always an important day in our house. When my parents got married, they made a vow that every Sunday would be a family day. Even before my sister and I were born, the two always spent the entire day together.

Dad often got teased at the docks because he wouldn't charter on Sundays. In the fishing business, most charter captains worked seven days a week, or when the weather was good and fish were biting. But Dad would always tell them, "The *Orca II* doesn't go out on Sundays."

Sunday was also important in our house because it meant our family went to church, no exceptions. We never missed church because faith was very important to our family. My dad was a leader and involved at church, and Mom helped teach the little kids' Sunday school class.

This Sunday I was extra tired from all the excitement of the day before and was having trouble waking up.

"Let's go, Casey. I let you sleep in. Church starts in 45 minutes," Mom called out as she pulled the blanket to the bottom of the bed.

I rolled over and pulled the covers back over my head. I was bummed Mom woke me up; I was just dreaming about the ocean.

I was still half asleep when Mom came back into my room.

"Get up, Casey! If you don't get up now, you might miss your opportunity to get some answers," she said.

Get some answers? What was Mom talking about? Was this just a ploy to get me out of bed? She could tell I wasn't taking her seriously.

"Okay, I guess figuring out your mystery from yesterday isn't very important to you."

As soon as she said that, I sat up wide awake.

It finally hit me what she was trying to hint at. *Bones...Bones usually sat three rows in front of us at church.* I jumped up and threw on some jeans and a thin pullover shirt.

"Not dressy enough...try again," Mom said when I entered the kitchen.

I hated dressing up, but at this point I was so excited to go to church, I quickly went back to my bedroom and put on a polo shirt.

I grabbed two pieces of toast on my way out and joined the rest of my family already waiting in our van. We had a short, ten-minute ride to church. All the way, I was trying to think of a way to ask Bones about yesterday without sounding nosey. Dad figured out what I was thinking about.

"Just ask him point blank; don't try to sneak or work around Bones. He's way too smart for that, and he isn't a patient person," Dad warned me.

We parked, rushed up the church's narrow staircase, and sat down just in time for the first song. Our church was one of the most beautiful I have ever seen. The windows overlooked Half Moon Bay, and the view was amazing. My parents told us they knew they had found their church the first time they had attended. Mom always said the view was as close to heaven as you could get without actually dying.

As we sat in the pew singing "The Old Rugged Cross," I scanned the pew where Bones usually sat.

No Bones…he isn't here! I let out a big sigh and continued to sing. Just as we started on the third verse, a movement to my left caught my eye. Sneaking into the pew was Bones.

His eyes met mine, and I could tell he knew I was looking for him. I quickly looked back towards the front of the church.

I knew it was just a matter of time before I was going to get the answer that I was looking for.

-10-

The sermon seemed to last forever because I was so anxious to talk to Bones. After the last prayer, families slowly started exiting to the back of the church.

I dodged through the crowd, trying to catch up to Bones before he left in his car. I sprinted through the parking lot and looked frantically for Bones' 1988 baby-blue Corvette. The car was almost as well-known as Bones himself.

One by one, each vehicle slowly pulled out of the church parking lot, but there was no blue Corvette.

"Casey!" a voice from the side of the church barked.

It was Bones, and he was walking towards me with his bicycle.

"Good day for a ride I thought," said Bones.

Bones' house was only a couple miles away, which probably made for a scenic, relaxing Sunday bike ride.

"How's it going?" he asked.

"Good…it's going good," I said.

"I had a feeling you were looking for me today at church," Bones said. He quickly added, "Can't get anything by me. Remember? I served in the Navy."

I nodded with a smile. *Remember? I was pretty sure there wasn't anyone around Half Moon Bay that hadn't heard a story about Bones' time in the Navy.*

"Yeah, I've been looking for you ever since you snuck out on me yesterday at the docks," I said. "Why did you look so concerned about the location of the cargo ship? Why do you care where it sunk?"

Bones looked across the road, his eyes fixed on the Pacific Ocean towards the Farallon Islands.

"You got a right to ask. I'm very curious about where that cargo ship went down," he said.

"But why?"

Bones started to stroke his chin, "I'll make you a deal. Talk your dad into taking us to the exact spot where the boat went down, and I'll tell you everything when we get there."

Dad wasn't going to break our Sunday family tradition very easily. I had to think of a way to talk him into taking the three of us back to the site of the sinking boat.

"Why don't you just ask him, Bones? My dad loves you," I said. I knew Dad, like most people in Half Moon Bay, was very fond of Bones. He was part of the town's history—someone people cared about.

"Can't do it, Casey. In fact, don't tell anyone that we talked or where we're going," warned Bones as he scanned the parking lot.

Bones is acting like we are being watched or recorded.

He added, "Promise me, Casey, the only one you'll tell is your dad."

Bones said it in way that wasn't rude or bossy, but more mysterious—like we were about to embark on some adventure. He said it in a way that didn't scare me; it just intrigued me.

"I'll meet you at the harbor at 2:00. Remember, just you and your dad—no one else needs to know," he added as he pedaled off on his bike.

Why 2:00? It was already around noon, which gave me less than two hours to convince my dad to take us back out.

As soon as our family got home, I rushed into my bedroom to change my clothes. I was running out of time and needed to think of a way to get Dad to take us out on the *Orca II*. Then I remembered the advice he had given me about talking to Bones—*Be honest and to the point.* So I called Dad into my room.

"Dad, I don't know what's going on, but Bones wants us to take him to the site where the cargo ship went down," I began. "The catch is we need to meet him at the dock in an hour."

Dad paused for a minute, and my mind raced with what he was thinking.

"Sure, let's do it. But, Casey, we can't make a habit of going out on the boat on Sundays," said Dad.

I wasn't the only one intrigued with Bones' interest in the sinking of the *S.S. Atlantis*.

-11-

When we pulled into the marina a few minutes early, Bones was already waiting for us at the boat. He stood leaning against the dock pole, and his posture was relaxed.

The three of us boarded the *Orca II*, anxious to explore the *Atlantis* wreckage and hear why Bones was so unusually concerned. I also couldn't get my mind off Monster. A part of me really wanted to encounter the giant shark again, but another part feared it.

While Dad and Bones were talking in the cabin of the boat, I was standing tall next to them, chest out. I wanted to look like I belonged with these two veterans of the sea.

"You okay, Casey?" Bones asked looking at me with a frown.

I guess I wasn't doing a very good job.

"Yeah, totally, I'm good," I replied and let out a sigh. I knew he could tell I was lying.

"You know, Casey, I was only 18 years old when I boarded an aircraft carrier, the *U.S.S. Independence* for the first time. It was August 10, 1945, and I was a young sailor looking for adventure," he said with a sly grin.

I smiled. This wasn't the first time that Bones would go off on some tangent and start telling Navy stories. In most cases, my mind would trail off when Bones started. But not today, this story was different. I felt like there was a bigger purpose to his story, and maybe it had something to do with our shark mystery.

We went out on deck and he continued, "Thought I was a goner many times, didn't think I would ever see my 21st birthday. Things were pretty scary back then when we were fighting the Japanese. The roughest battle came that March off the island of Okinawa. Our job was supplying torpedoes and dive bombers, and we stayed in the action until early June."

While the story was interesting, I was wondering what this had to do with our mystery or was Bones taking advantage of me being stuck on the boat with him?

Bones went on to tell me they had eventually helped lead air strikes on the Japan mainland. That fall, the *U.S.S. Independence* aided surveillance flights over the mainland by locating prisoner of war camps. In September, the ship left Tokyo, traveled around Saipan and Guam, and arrived back in San Francisco on October 31.

"That was yesterday," I quickly said.

"Isn't that a strange coincidence?" he asked.

"That fall I was transferred off the ship. Over the next three years, I had various assignments on other aircraft carriers, but I never forgot the adventures I had on the *Independence*."

Whenever he mentioned the ship, his tone shifted. It was obvious the ship had a lot of sentimental value to Bones; his voice quivered as if the aircraft carrier were a part of his family.

The hour trip to visit the sunken *S.S. Atlantis* seemed to go by fast as we listened to Bones' stories. I was totally mesmerized by his tales of the gutty performance of the *U.S.S. Independence*.

"That sounds like an awesome ship. Have you ever gone back to visit it? I wonder where it's at now," I said.

Bones turned to look back toward the shoreline and replied in a grim voice, "We're closer to the old girl than you think…" He turned away and walked back into the cabin.

-12-

I waited a minute or so and then followed Bones inside. I was hoping he was going to finish his story so I could find out what had happened to the *U.S.S. Independence.* I didn't have time to ask him when the motor suddenly slowed and began to idle in the middle of nowhere. "Here we are. Not sure what you're looking for, Bones. There's just a little leftover gas and oil here," Dad said.

I went to the side and looked over the edge. A strange greenish film floated on top of the water. It looked different than the spill that was around the boat when it had sunk. Bones looked over the edge, observing the greenish pigments that penetrated the blue Pacific waters.

Bones dropped his head in disappointment. "That's not gas or oil," said Bones.

"What is it?' Dad quickly asked.

"We need to return to Half Moon as quickly as possible," Bones said.

"This boat isn't moving an inch until you tell us what's going on," Dad said sternly.

The accelerator on the boat was still idling. The *Orca II* was floating in the giant green film; it was everywhere. Bones knew something; this wasn't from the *Atlantis* wreck.

Dad and I just stood staring, waiting for Bones to educate us on what the green film was.

"What's that?" asked Bones pointing towards the horizon at a black object floating 500 yards off the ship.

At first I thought he was pointing towards the rocky outline of the Farallon Islands. Then I spotted the object floating in the waves, but this time it was much closer to our location.

Our boat was still about ten miles or so from the islands as Dad cranked the engine and headed towards the mysterious object floating through the green ooze. As the boat motored closer and closer, I recognized it.

"It's the dead blue whale," I said as Dad started to slow the engines. The boat was about 100 yards away when the entire carcass disappeared, popping back up seconds later.

"She's still here," I said to Dad.

"*She?* What are you talking about?" asked Bones.

The whale looked way different in just one day. A huge portion of it had been totally eaten, and large bite marks could be seen on both sides of the animal. The large blue whale looked to be half the size it was the previous day. The whale was covered in the same greenish goo from the shipwreck site. The green liquid had attached itself to the entire creature. The carcass bobbed up once again, but this time we were close enough to see underneath the animal.

If Bones was still questioning who "she" was, he wasn't anymore.

Monster's indented dorsal fin crested the water briefly before the animal ripped out a huge piece of the blue whale.

The two distinct notches in Monster's dorsal fin made the shark easy to recognize. A shark's dorsal fin is like a human fingerprint; each one has its own unique dorsal fin.

The strange thing was this shark was even bigger than the one I had seen the day before; it had to be at least 22 feet long. *How could two sharks with the exact same dorsal fin be feeding on the whale?*

Impossible! This couldn't be the same shark! There was no way a shark could grow that much in just one day.

"That's the biggest white shark I've ever seen," stammered Bones. That was a huge statement because in all of Bones' crazy sea adventures, he had seen plenty of great whites.

Bones turned to my dad. "I've seen enough. We need to get out of here fast!"

Dad took the not-so-subtle hint and cranked the motor, turning the *Orca II* east, plotting our course back to Half Moon Bay.

I stared at the shark feeding frenzy until it was just a dot on the horizon and remained lost in thought at the size and power of the shark.

LANE WALKER

Were there two huge great white sharks living in the waters of Northern California? Did Monster have a twin?

- 13 -

The three of us sat quietly in the cabin of the *Orca II* while Dad floored the accelerator.

"I was afraid this would happen someday," Bones uttered as he finally broke the silence.

"I think it's time you tell us what in the world is going on," Dad demanded.

Bones took a deep breath and began, "In 1945 the *U.S.S. Independence* was part of Operation Crossroads, an atomic experiment held between Hawaii and Australia. The United States government wanted to see how a naval ship would hold up to an atomic blast. The *Independence* was placed one-half mile from the blast. But the old girl didn't sink in the blast, so the Navy decided to decommission the ship and sink her. The hull of the ship was highly radioactive and moved first to Pearl Harbor, then to San Francisco Bay, and then to its final resting place here among the giant great white sharks off the Farallon Islands. They floated the ship and shot two torpedoes right into the hull, sending the ship to a watery eternal grave," said Bones.

"You're telling us your ship—the aircraft carrier that you served on in Japan—was used in an atomic blast experiment and was later sunk off the shores of the Farallon Islands?" I asked without stopping for a breath. This was like something out of a fairy tale—almost too crazy to be real.

"That's exactly what I'm telling you," Bones replied with a serious expression on his face.

"Okay, so what does that have to do with the sunken cargo ship and the sighting of Monster?" Dad insisted.

"After getting out of the Navy, I settled near Old Moon Bay. I wanted to be close to my old ship; it was special to me in so many ways. I don't know how to explain it, but for me I always had be close to the old girl," Bones explained.

"So that's why you were so concerned when you heard the Mayday calls of the *Atlantis* over the radio? You were worried it would disturb the final resting place of the *Independence*?" I asked.

"No, the ship is located a couple miles northeast of here. She's close, but I knew those coordinates weren't hers. The old girl isn't dangerous anyway; the radiation levels are very low now and pose no harm to the ocean," Bones explained.

Radiation levels? Secret location of a sunken World War II aircraft carrier? There was much more to Bones than the old, gray-haired man let people see.

"When I heard coordinates of the ship, my heart sank. I was hoping you'd gotten the numbers messed up or were a couple miles off course," Bones said.

But that wasn't the case. The crash coordinates were accurate. Bones just had to see it for himself.

"I have lived in fear for years that something like this could happen," said Bones. "And now it is."

No doubt about it, Bones was still a mystery.

-14-

Bones' real name was Earl Wright. He was born and raised on the coastal waters of Florida on the Gulf of Mexico. He grew up a loner, living with his single dad who worked most of the time.

The day Earl graduated from high school, his dad gave him three options—Army, Navy, or Air Force. Having lived on the water his entire life, it was a natural choice for him to join the Navy. In school, math and problem solving came easy for Earl. When it came time to pick his job choice, naval engineering seemed like a great fit. After six months of training and boot camp at Great Lakes, Earl Wright was sent to serve on the *U.S.S. Independence.*

Earl adjusted quickly to the rigors of boot camp, and the need for discipline and responsibility came natural. The only thing he struggled with was the food—he hated it. In fact, he found it repulsive and only ate the minimal amount needed to survive. By the end of boot camp, Earl had dropped 30 pounds and was super skinny. That's when Earl Wright became Bones, and the nickname stuck. Everyone, including his dad, called him Bones.

In those times, boys went into the service and they came home men—if they were lucky enough to come home at all. World War II was raging and working on an aircraft carrier was dangerous business. Bones served his four years without incident and was excited to start a life after the Navy.

When his military time was up, he traveled around the country but had never found a place to call home. One night while staring at the moon, he thought about the last place that he had called home. He didn't think about where he grew up in Florida. His mind wandered to his time on the *Independence*, so he made up his mind to find her again. After discovering what had happened to his old ship, Bones settled in Old Moon Bay. He picked it because no matter what direction from his front window he looked, he would be looking in the ship's direction.

Bones never married, but he loved to fish and spent most of his days telling stories and hanging out at the docks at Half Moon Bay or watching the surfers at the Mavericks.

It was his job after the Navy that had the old man so worried.

-15-

When Bones first arrived in Half Moon Bay, he was poor and jobless. At first, he spent most of his days fishing the public pier in Pillar Point Harbor, hoping to catch enough for a dinner.

The water around the pier was mostly shallow and had a muddy bottom. He became an expert at catching perch, flatfish, starry flounder, and rockfish. It was on Pillar Point pier that he met a man named Mr. Hudson. As fate would have it, Mr. Hudson was looking for someone with an engineering background. He was a manager for the Atomic Energy Commission, more commonly known as the A.E.C.

The A.E.C. had started out as an agency of the

United States government formed by President Harry Truman to foster and control atomic science and energy. Over time, the power of the A.E.C. was shifted from the military into civilian hands. The shift had given the A.E.C. complete control with little oversight over the plants, laboratories, equipment, and personnel that had been used during the war to produce the atomic bomb.

Later, the A.E.C. shifted their operations to include controlling radiation dangers, ecosystem development, and ecology. Funding was dedicated to research and numerous environmental projects in the Arctic and across the Pacific Ocean. The A.E.C. projects were designed to create peaceful applications and deal with the disposal of atomic energy.

Bones started working at the A.E.C. towards the end of the biggest environmental disposal project in the history of the company. Between 1946 and 1970, the A.E.C. strategically dumped over 47,000 large containers of radioactive waste.

The waste was stored in 55-gallon drums and cemented to ensure they would sink to the bottom.

The drop point was in the Gulf of the Farallones, just miles from the Farallon Islands.

Bones had been in charge of mapping their final dumping zone to ensure a safe depth and location. On the day of one scheduled dump, bad weather had rolled into San Francisco Bay. He begged his boss to wait until clear weather, but his concerns fell on deaf ears.

The A.E.C. dumping crew was given the exact coordinates where the dumping was to occur. They set out on a large barge, full of drums of nuclear waste. About an hour into the trip, the weather had worsened. When the barge had started to take on water and struggle in the waves, the barge captain made a horrible decision. He figured they were far enough out to sea and instructed his men to dump the remaining barrels. Due to the captain's fear of sinking, hundreds of barrels of dangerous radioactive waste were dumped in water that was too shallow to contain them forever.

Today off the coast of California, not far from San Francisco Bay, hundreds of barrels of radioactive waste lay dormant at the bottom of the Pacific

---

Ocean. The A.E.C. covered up the event and included the barrels in the report so it looked as though they were dumped with all the other ones in much deeper water. Their plan had worked for over 50 years.

"I was young in my career and should have done more. I have lived in fear for all these years, waiting for our mistake to haunt us. The time has come; we are about to pay for our mistake," Bones told Dad and me.

He took a deep breath and added, "When the *Atlantis* sank, the weight of the granite crashed to the sea floor. I am convinced it broke open hundreds of barrels of dangerous radioactive waste that is now leaking and filling the water around the crash site with dangerous nuclear waste."

What? Radioactive waste in our backyard?

Dad and I couldn't think of any more questions to ask and so we concentrated on starting the engine and heading for home.

-16-

It was late afternoon when we arrived back at the docks at Half Moon Bay. As we pulled in, I was shocked at how busy the marina had gotten.

"Dad, do you think people know about Monster?" I asked.

"I don't know, son, but it seems like something is going on."

Bones was pacing back and forth at the front of the bow. I could tell he was filled with both fear and guilt. He heard Dad and I talking and rushed towards us.

"No one knows, and they can't know. I have to find a way to fix it. I know what will happen if they find out," Bones snapped.

He looked towards the crowded dock and suddenly looked even more tense. "They aren't here for your shark or that boat that sank. They're here for the Mavericks! That could mean disaster!"

The Mavericks FROTH Surfing Championship was one of the largest, most dangerous surfing competitions in the world. Every year during the first weekend in November, tens of thousands of tourists and thrill seekers came to Pillar Point Harbor, which was only a three-mile drive north of Half Moon Bay.

This year's contest was going to be the largest Mavericks' event ever and couldn't have come at a worse time. The last thing Monster needed was a bunch of tourists in the water and boats cruising off the coast.

Billionaire business tycoon Lance Biggs was sponsoring the event. There was a cash prize of $500,000 to anyone that could ride the left side of Mavericks for 20 seconds.

Biggs was a superstar is his own right and his own mind. He was a former extreme sports surfer turned businessman after he broke his leg during a surfing competition off Maui, which ended his career. While in the hospital, Biggs had an idea to market a new drink he had invented—FROTH.

In surfing terms, *froth* is the foam left over after a wave crashes. Surfers would love to hit the froth, so Biggs incorporated the name into his energy drink.

Earlier in Biggs' surfing career, he loved to chase giant waves all over the world. Sleep wasn't high on his priority list. He needed something to keep him going hard on the waves, so he had invented the special drink. He was a surfing legend and a great marketer, so the popularity of his energy drink exploded. Everyone along the West Coast, surfer or not, started drinking his flavored FROTH.

After the original version, Biggs came out with other flavors in the FROTH line, including grape, piña colada, lemon lime, and cola. The main ingredients in FROTH were caffeine and buckets of sugar.

I had no idea what they tasted like since my parents said they were unhealthy and totally off limits. It seemed like everywhere you went in Southern California, FROTH signs littered the beautiful landscape. It was even worse around Half Moon Bay over the past three weeks. Around every corner and attached to almost every business was a yellow and red FROTH sign.

What had started out as a hobby for Biggs while he was laid up from his injury, turned into a billion-dollar business. Shortly afterward, he hung up his professional surfboard to focus on FROTH. Now he was one of the most recognizable celebrities in California.

Biggs' cash prize of $500,000 was bringing a lot of money as well as a ton of people to the local businesses. All of the local hotels, tour boats, and restaurants were booked the entire week before Saturday's competition. The local docks were getting overrun with boats and tourists looking for the best place to watch the Mavericks competition.

The prize money would surely bring a record number of surfers and tourists to the Mavericks. Unfortunately, great white sharks weren't the only killers stalking the murky waters around Half Moon Bay.

- 17 -

The strong fall winds slam into the jagged, underwater rocky edges of the shoreline at the Mavericks. Waves can crest at over 25 feet and top out at over 60 feet. The sound is so loud and deafening, it can be measured on a seismometer. Surfers ride and enjoy the Mavericks year around, but certain waters, at the most dangerous point near Pillar Point, are closed from October through March.

The rumor around town was that Biggs spent over a million dollars to lobby the local county officials to host the Mavericks November FROTH Surfing Championship and open up the most dangerous section of the Mavericks for the competition. In the end, Biggs used his money and power to get his way, allowing the event to happen.

Riding any wave on the Mavericks coast is dangerous, but only the most elite could ride the "left." Biggs put the $500,000 cash prize money on the "left."

What makes the left side at Mavericks so dangerous is that the waves are unreliable. It is a much faster run and typically shoots riders out of a quicker pipe barrel, flipping most of them furiously off their boards.

The longest recorded ride on the left at the Mavericks was twenty seconds by Luke Longway, a surfing legend from the 1980s. Biggs' cash prize was simple—ride the left side of Mavericks for twenty-one seconds and go home with $500,000.

Before contestants could compete, Biggs had each one sign a waiver not holding him or FROTH energy drinks responsible for harm or death. Last year alone, two professional surfers who snuck out to try to ride the Mavericks on Christmas Eve never opened their Christmas presents. Both men died in their failed attempt to ride the left at Mavericks.

"This isn't good," Bones mumbled as we pulled into our private dock. "No matter what happens, we can't tell anyone about the radioactive waste or the huge shark. I have to figure out what we can do before this gets out."

I listened to Bones and tried to figure out what he was most worried about—people finding out about his role in dumping nuclear radioactive waste near the Farallon Islands or the fact that there was a world record white shark not far off the shoreline the same week as the Mavericks event.

"Bones, this isn't right; we can't keep this a secret. Someone could get badly hurt," Dad informed him.

"Just give me 24 hours, please. I promise I'll have a plan by then," Bones pleaded.

"You have until tomorrow at 5:00 p.m., and then we're going to notify the sheriff's office," Dad stated firmly.

"Fine, fine, do whatever you think you need to do. But don't say a word to anyone, I mean anyone, until tomorrow," Bones demanded.

———

With that, Bones scooted off the boat and disappeared among the mass of visitors at the docks. As hard as it would be, Dad and I would keep our word. Bones needed some time to think and come up with a plan.

Little did I know our promise didn't matter.

-18-

Dad was pretty quiet on the way home from the marina. I could tell he was thinking about the options in case Bones' plan didn't work. We pulled into the driveway, and after Dad put his truck into park, he grabbed my arm.

"I want you to know that this really bothers me," he said with a frown.

Dad was always the happiest when he was on the open water of the ocean. Even though he had spent over half his life on the ocean, there wasn't a day that went by that Dad didn't appreciate the ocean.

Most men would have seen Monster as a beast—a true killer. Sharks have a reputation as man eaters, but my dad didn't see the shark as a savage killer. He knew that we were entering the shark's world.

"I know that, Dad," I said.

"My biggest fear is what would happen if people found out there's a 22-foot great white shark feeding between Half Moon Bay and the Farallon Islands. With all the press and tourists in town for the Mavericks thing, it would be bad, son. They'll try to kill that shark."

Fear and a lack of understanding about great white sharks would lead to big problems for Monster. I was nervous too about the radioactive waste and the effects it could have on marine life. If the crash site were contaminated, there was no telling the damage it could cause.

"We'll give Bones until tomorrow, and then we'll call the authorities or whoever we need to call."

I nodded in agreement.

We strolled into the house to the delicious smell of Mom's meatloaf. The aroma was so wonderful, especially after spending all day on the ocean. The table was set and dinner was waiting, but there was no sight of Mom or Sara.

Dad went into his bedroom to change and headed towards the basement. I could faintly hear voices coming from the family room.

They must have heard me coming down the steps. I was greeted with Mom yelling, "Casey, Casey get in here!"

I jogged a couple steps and turned down the hallway leading to our family room.

"You have to see this YouTube video that Channel 6 just aired," cried Sara.

I turned into the family room and towards the television set. I was met with the image of a huge shark ripping apart a giant blue whale and men shouting in Spanish. I suddenly realized that one of the four *Atlantis*' crewman had taken a video of the giant shark, and now it was posted on social media.

It was Monster, and I knew the shark wasn't a secret anymore.

-19-

Monday was my least favorite day of the week. It meant I had a long wait before I could fish again.

It was hard to sit at a desk all day after spending most of my time during the weekend fishing and exploring the waters of the Pacific. Even though I was only in eighth grade, I knew that my future would be lived out on the water and not sitting behind a computer or desk all day.

Dad and the *Orca II* were set to have a busy week. Dad was booked in advance with lots of fishing trips. Most tourists were in town to enjoy some saltwater fishing before attending the Mavericks FROTH Surfing Championship on Saturday.

The majority of Dad's clients booked salmon

charters. I knew most of Dad's routine and where he fished for certain species. Salmon were big, strong fish, and anglers loved to fight them. They also taste great and are easy to clean.

Salmon fishing would take my dad north, not east towards the Farallon Islands. The water where Dad usually fished for salmon was much closer to shore, only four to six miles off the coast.

November fishing off the Farallon Islands was so intense, it often scared the average fisherman. The two-hour trip to the Farallon Islands in November isn't for the weak. The weather is usually cold, and the waves can make even experienced seamen sick. Plus, the idea of fishing in a great white shark hotbed usually scared off a lot of clients.

This morning Dad left early, well before 5:00 a.m. to get the *Orca II* ready for a bunch of doctors who had flown in from Detroit for a medical conference in San Francisco. They were all novice fisherman and nervous about fishing the Pacific, so they didn't want to go too far off the coastline. In fact, the doctor that booked the trip said they wanted to be close enough to shore to swim if they had to.

Getting up for school was a struggle for me. I was tired, and my mind was all over the place. When I got to school, I noticed there was a unique buzz in the hallways. Everyone was talking about the shark video that had gone viral and the surfing event at Mavericks.

During lunch I watched a group of seventh grade boys in a circle at the end of a lunchroom table. They were huddled tight and watching a cell phone. When I stood behind them and listened for a minute, I could tell they were watching the video of Monster. They started saying horrible things about killing the shark and what they would do if they found the giant great white.

A part of me was proud as they talked about the shark, knowing that I had come eye to eye with the giant just two days earlier.

"Look at that thing! What a killer!" one of the boys remarked.

"That shark is too big! Imagine what it would do to a boat! It would eat the whole thing and kill everyone aboard," said another boy.

I just rolled my eyes in disgust. *Did these idiots*

actually think Monster would eat a boat and then eat everyone on board? They acted like the shark was some mass murderer craving human blood. They had no idea about the subtle beauty of Monster. They had no clue how rare and special a great white shark like that was.

"I hope the Navy sends a ship out and shoots a missile at that shark. They need to need to kill it!" said one of the boys.

I couldn't handle it anymore, I reached down and ripped the phone out of his hand. I was so angry. After seeing the size of the shark, fear and hysteria were making these kids hate it.

They just sat and stared at me; they could tell I was mad, and they didn't want to mess with an upset eighth grader. I walked out of the lunchroom and dropped the phone in one of the trash barrels.

"What's his problem?" one of the boys whispered to the others.

"I don't know, but my sister is going to kill me. That's her new phone, and now it's covered in meatball sauce," said another.

I didn't care what they thought. It was obvious

they were immature, dumb seventh graders who had absolutely no clue about sharks. They needed an education about the Pacific—especially about great white sharks.

-20-

Every day after school I had the same routine. As soon as I got home, I would jump on my bike and ride the mile down to Half Moon Bay marina to wait for Dad to come in from his afternoon charter fishing trip. I always kept a couple poles and a tackle box in the back of his truck so I could fish off the docks. I tried to get in at least a good hour of fishing before Dad's boat returned.

There was good fishing at the marina, and I knew exactly where to catch them. I loved to catch surf perch, jack smelt, and rock fish.

When I arrived at the marina that day, I was surprised to see Dad's boat already sitting in the boat slip. I noticed him talking with a group of men and figured they were the doctors from the charter trip.

I grabbed my pole and went around the end of the dock to a little inlet. It didn't take long before I had caught about five fish; the bite was good, and I was enjoying every second. When I hold the rod and pull it back to cast, I feel strong. I feel complete.

I wasn't fishing for long before I heard Dad's familiar whistle signaling me back to the truck.

"Hey, Dad, short trip?" I asked when I returned.

"Yeah, we really hammered the salmon, limited out by 3:00 p.m. The bite was hot; we caught a fish almost every third cast," Dad said quickly.

His voice seemed a little irritated, and I didn't know why since the fishing trip was such a huge success.

"I wanted to talk to you before Bones gets here," Dad said. Bones was supposed to meet us in the parking lot at 5:00 p.m. to go over his plan.

"Dad, I saw you talking to those guys. Were they the guys you took fishing?" I asked.

"No. No, they weren't, son. They were asking me about chartering a trip," responded Dad.

"Oh, cool," I replied.

"No, not cool, Casey. Those men were associates of Mr. Biggs. They wanted to pay me a lot of money to help them find a certain shark."

After the video footage of the giant shark was aired on television, I was sure people from all over the coast would want to catch a glimpse of the shark. I couldn't figure out what made Dad upset.

"They don't want to just see the shark. They want to make sure she isn't a problem for this weekend's surfing event," Dad explained.

"Why? The shark is over an hour off shore; she doesn't have any interest in surfers at Point Pillar," I replied.

"I know that, and you know that, Casey, but I think Mr. Biggs would go to any lengths to ensure his surfing competition takes place. The last thing he wants is people scared to get in the water this weekend."

This type of man-eating shark hysteria was nothing new to my dad.

"Son, I've seen this happen before, and it doesn't bode well for the shark."

I knew what he was talking about. Dad often told me about his childhood and growing up in Martha's Vineyard in the post-*Jaws* days.

While the movie was a huge hit in pop culture, some really bad things happened to sharks because of it. The film created a global nightmare for sharks. It especially hit home for my dad because people all along the East Coast had shark mania. Fisherman and thrill seekers wanted to prove how brave they were, so they set out in small boats to find sharks.

The perception was that these sharks cruised the shoreline craving human flesh. We now know how untrue that is, but at the time, people believed it. Tens of thousands of sharks were killed after the release of the movie because of people's fears.

Over the years, most of that mindset has changed—thanks to scientific research and education. While shark attacks still occur, the odds of that happening are small.

When I was in sixth grade, we had to do a persuasive essay on something we were passionate about. I did mine on sharks, and during my research, I found out that more people are killed taking a selfie than those attacked by a shark. I don't see people trying to outlaw cell phones.

"Anytime fear drives a human decision, bad things happen," Dad said. "We venture into the ocean—into a shark's habitat. What do people expect will happen?"

-21-

Dad's watch beeped loudly as it did every day at 5:00 p.m. He did this as a helpful reminder that he needed to end the conversations at the fishing pier. Fisherman are known to have a gift of gab and can tell stories late into the night. When Dad first began his business, he used to come home late all the time and miss dinner.

"Here he comes," Dad said.

I turned and saw Bones propping his bike against the wall of the bait shop.

"I have some good news and some bad news," Bones began.

In my experience, it's usually all bad news when someone started off talking like that.

"Good news first," Dad said.

"I made a phone call to an old friend I worked with at the A.E.C. and told him about the radioactive waste leaking. I told him the overall general size of the waste cloud in the water, and he figured 30 to 40 barrels were busted open when the *Atlantis* sank. He also said the waste would be diluted pretty quickly based on water flow and currents in the Pacific, so there shouldn't be a huge impact on the ocean environment. In fact, we were probably the last people to see it before it was gone," explained Bones.

"That is good news; now what's the bad?"

Bones rubbed his hands, rocking back and forth showing his nerves.

"The bad news is that when I told him about the whale carcass and the giant white shark, he got nervous. He said that top secret studies have shown that nuclear waste can cause erratic growth patterns," said Bones.

That would explain why the shark seemed so much bigger than the day before.

"That's not too bad," I finally spoke up.

"They don't know the exact effect on the shark, but they want to, and there's only one way for them to find out," Bones said softly.

"No! Absolutely not," Dad said quickly.

"It's the only way, Corey," Bones said, turning towards my dad. "They want to find the shark and bring it into the lab to study the effects of the radioactive waste. You know how this has got to end," Bones said.

They planned on killing the shark! The Atomic Energy Commission's past mistake meant they would have to kill Monster. The shark was going to pay with its life to cover up their mistake!

It seemed like Monster didn't stand much of a chance. The locals were afraid of the shark, Mr. Biggs didn't want him to ruin his surfing competition, and the A.E.C. wanted to kill the shark for research.

Bones leaned in closer to us. "The other thing is, I'd be extra careful. They don't want any of the news about the nuclear waste stuff getting out. I assured them that I was the only one who knew, but I don't trust them. They'll do anything to keep this out of the press, and I mean *anything*," Bones said, looking over his shoulder.

"Is that a threat?" Dad asked.

"Corey, it's a clear warning. Be careful, don't trust anyone, and keep what we saw to yourself—that's all," Bones advised us.

-22-

On the way home Dad called his clients and cancelled the fishing charter that was scheduled for the next morning.

"What are we going to do? We have to stop them from killing Monster," I said.

"I know, but that video is going to make it tough. I have a suspicion that every tour boat in the marina will be looking for the giant shark, plus the A.E.C. and every boat in the Biggs arsenal," Dad said as he shook his head.

He added, "I'm going to need you tomorrow. You're going to have to miss school."

Sweet. There was a sense of pride knowing that Dad had chosen me to help him on this adventure, plus I had an Algebra quiz that I hadn't studied for.

Dad excused himself from dinner that night, saying he had an important phone call to make. It was later in the evening, around 8:30 by the time he returned from the basement.

The television was on, and we were watching the preview for Monday Night Football.

I could hear Dad coming up the steps when the football announcer was drowned out by the voice of my favorite NFL player, quarterback for the San Francisco 49ers, Jim Jefferson.

"Hang ten and grab a can of FROTH this weekend on your way to the Mavericks for the FROTH Surfing Championship," he announced.

Okay, now Jim Jefferson was my *former* favorite player. The thought of the Mavericks surfing event made my stomach roll. Biggs had so much money and advertising into the event, the chance of a giant shark in the area wasn't going to stop it—even if he had to kill it.

I shut off the television and walked into the kitchen to talk to Dad.

"What's the plan?" I asked.

"There's only thing we can do," said Dad.

"And that is?"

"We have to find Monster before anyone else and keep him as far away from Half Moon Bay and Pillar Point as possible."

Dad went on to tell me that the phone call he made was to an old friend, Dr. Robert Lott. He has known Dr. Lott for over twenty years and talked to him several times each year.

Only a handful of scientists and researchers live on the Farallon Islands. They work for Point Blue Conservation and monitor wildlife trends on the island. The islands are home to over 400 species of birds, with an estimated 250,000 birds living on the island. Other than the workers, the rest of the island is closed with no public access. Lucky for us, Dr. Lott was one of the wildlife biologists who currently lived in the one house there.

"That's great, but isn't his job researching the birds on the island?" I asked. I was confused as to how he was going to be able to help.

"His main job on the island is monitoring sea-bird migration and habitat on the island, but that's not all he does. A couple years ago, we worked together tagging great white sharks around Farallon," Dad said. "He still has one tag left from our shark-tagging mission, and I plan on getting it and putting it on Monster."

There were only three people who knew exactly where the whale carcass was, so we were hoping that Monster was still in the vicinity. Even though Bones knew too, we were hoping that he didn't give away the shark's location. It was the only insurance policy keeping him alive with the A.E.C.

"If we can tag the shark, at least we'll know where he is and if he's close to Half Moon Bay. We can use the tag to keep Monster safe. The only problem is, we have to go pick it up," Dad explained.

While it sounded easy, I knew it wouldn't be. We couldn't just drive over to Dr. Lott's house and grab the tracking tag. Dr. Lott lived full time on the Farallon Islands. Getting there was challenging enough. It was going to be even trickier with the addition of all the boats in the water for the Mavericks championship.

The real challenge would be once we got to the islands. There was no way to sneak onto the islands. There's only one way to reach the research lab. To gain access to South Farrallon Island, the passenger has to transfer to a smaller boat and maneuver through a maze of rocks and hazards. Then a crane is used to lift the boat 50 feet over the ocean onto a rocky landing ledge.

The thought of paddling through shark-infested waters was terrifying enough. But the idea of being lifted by a crane over the same waters was pure madness.

-23-

That night I barely slept. Every time I started to drift off to sleep, I imagined the giant jaws of Monster feeding and ripping apart the blue whale.

In my dream I couldn't imagine what a shark like that could do to us as the crane dangled us above the water. It was about 3:00 a.m. when I finally figured out I was obsessing about the shark like everyone around town and finally fell asleep.

The next morning my alarm went off earlier than usual. Dad wanted this to be a covert mission, so he planned to get on the water before any of the other boats. Bones' message was clear—be careful. It's an eerie feeling thinking some government agency might be watching our every move.

We arrived at the marina around 4:00 a.m. welcomed by the soft white glow of the parking lot lights. I was tired and hadn't slept well all week. Dad could tell as he watched me wipe the sleep from my eyes several times.

"Do you want me to grab you one of those? I heard they will really wake you up," Dad said as he sarcastically pointed at a FROTH sign on the side of the restaurant. Dad knew how to motivate me for a mission. I was suddenly wide awake and alert.

Dad had been to the Farallon Islands so many times, he could do it blindfolded. When we got out of the truck, I noticed it was a windy morning. I glanced over at the flag on top of Blackbeard's Ghost, a popular seafood restaurant in the marina. The wind was pushing the flag in every direction, making a loud popping sound.

"Looks like a west, southwest wind. Not the greatest to visit Farallon," Dad noted as we headed towards the *Orca II*.

Dad has fished in every kind of weather imaginable, but he never had to get into a smaller boat and get lifted onto the Farallon Islands. A west, southwest wind meant it would blow directly towards the rocky cliffs of the islands. The biology station, which was the only active house on the islands, was located on South Farallon Island, making the trek even more dangerous.

When we got to the *Orca II*, I started my pre-trip checks while Dad paced back and forth on the boat. It was obvious he was second-guessing our trip this morning. We both knew that it was now or never. If we didn't get the satellite tag on Monster, the shark was in big trouble. The rest of the week, Ultimate Saltwater Adventures was booked with large groups fishing near San Francisco Bay. The A.E.C. and Lance Biggs were going to be in hot pursuit of Monster. The Mavericks FROTH event was only four days away. Our time to get in the water and help Monster was now; we couldn't wait another day.

Dad had reminded me to be in stealth mode with no lights and as quiet as possible. It was harder fumbling around in the dark, but it meant we could get out of the marina unseen. Just as I was taking off the last tie down rope, I heard a loud noise coming from the parking lot. Looking up at the empty lot, I noticed a brand-new black truck and trailer under the parking lot lights. It was 4:15 a.m.—early for even the most diehard anglers to be launching a boat. It was strange, since most charter captains didn't arrive until 5:30 a.m.

"Cast off the line, Casey; we need to go now!" Dad whispered.

Dad made sure all the cabin and running lights were shut off on the *Orca II*. Besides being windy, there must have been low hanging clouds because there was almost no visibility. I had never tried to untie the boat in the dark without any lights, and it proved to be challenging. Dad waited until the truck started backing down to the boat ramp before turning the key to the ignition. He kept the throttle low and quiet as we moved out of the docks to the open water of the marina.

Whoever was at the boat ramp wasn't going to be able to follow the *Orca II* today. I glanced back one more time as we crossed the last no wake buoy in the harbor. The huge black boat was in the water almost ready to launch. We had managed to get out without them noticing. I sat at the back of the boat and was thankful for the darkness.

Safely out of the harbor, Dad pushed the accelerator and flipped on the lights. Looking behind as we sped away, the lights off the coast looked like fireflies. The wind was at our back, so the drive to the Farallon Islands would go much quicker this morning.

The slapping sound of the waves hitting the boat and the lack of sleep from the night before created a perfect combination, and I nodded off to the taste of sea spray. I felt like I had slept for weeks when Dad's cold hand shook me awake. I wiped the drool from my jacket. I had slept the entire trip to the islands.

Still groggy, I squinted towards the front of the boat. In the distance, jagged rock formations broke through the thick fog. The sun was starting to peek through the clouds and cast a shade of light on the foggy island. It looked like a watercolor painting as the colorful hues met the dark, drab colors of the island.

The island had many folk tales and much history surrounding it. Early settlers to San Francisco believed that the fog was God's way of protecting the island from people. No one usually dared to access the island in the dangerous November wind and fog. As the boat drifted closer and closer to the island, it was obvious we weren't the only ones up early. There were loud splashes and noises surrounding the boat in all directions.

Numerous northern elephant seals were super active in the water. I had never been so close to the islands, since we always fished about a half mile off shore. Dad cut the main engine and used the wind to pilot the *Orca II* towards the dangerous shores. The fog was dense, but Dad used our onboard GPS to guide the boat to the correct spot.

The boat jerked as Dad dropped the anchor. It was pretty light out by then, and I could tell we were about 200 yards from the island in much shallower water. It was still windy, but the cliffs and rocky edges of the island helped block some of it.

"Okay, you wait here, Casey. It should take about

an hour for me to get what we need and be back," Dad ordered.

An hour alone in the middle of shark-infested waters surrounded by elephant seals?

I could tell Dad was nervous, but he tried to act like his crane ride up to the island would be easy. "One of the conditions with Dr. Lott was that I had to meet him on the island, since his contract with his company doesn't allow him to leave," said Dad. "I'll be fine, and so will you. We need that tracker."

Dad wasn't much for talking about things; he was an action guy. He gave me a quick hug and climbed into the *Little Minnow*, a much smaller lifeboat we always carried on the side of the *Orca II*. The boat was seldom used but was there in case of emergencies. Sometimes Dad would let me take it round the marina and fish some of the small inlets and fishing holes.

My nerves were maxed out as I watched wave after wave engulf Dad and the smaller boat while he motored towards the crane. The *Little Minnow* looked so tiny on the ocean; in fact, Monster was bigger than the entire lifeboat!

Getting closer and closer, he was about thirty feet from the crane when I saw the first dorsal fin cresting the water. Within seconds, two more fins appeared. Dad had three great white sharks circling him in the *Little Minnow*. It seems like our mission wasn't so secret after all—the sharks were curious as to who was in their water.

This trip was getting more and more dangerous. Having elephant seals all around us and great white sharks looking for their breakfast was a bad combination.

When Dad reached his landing spot, there was an attachment for the boat waiting for him. Dad fumbled and took a couple of minutes, but eventually he hooked up the small lifeboat to the rope. Almost on cue, the crane turned on, pulling the *Little Minnow* out of the water towards the top of the island.

I was alone on the *Orca II*.

-24-

The wind howled, and the waves crashed over the *Orca's* hull. The salty ocean sea spray soaked me, but I couldn't sit in the cabin.

This was probably the first time in my life that hoped I didn't see any great white sharks. I slowly walked around the boat, scanning the murky waters, looking for any sign of a shark.

While sharks, especially great white sharks, can be dangerous to humans, most attacks were a matter of mistaken identity—surfers mistaken for seals—or sharks being curious.

The morning sunshine was a welcome sight, as the yellow light broke through what little fog was left. Visibility was much better, and I could see clearly in all directions. Off to my left, near Seal Rock, there was a huge mass of elephant seals. They were pretty noisy. I wondered if they were celebrating not becoming breakfast for a great white.

The buzzing sound of the crane shifted my attention back towards the island. The *Little Minnow* was on its way back down the crane. The crane creaked and moaned the entire time, but within minutes the small lifeboat was back in the water. Heading into the wind towards the *Orca II* took a little longer, but eventually the little boat pulled up alongside.

Both boats were rocking in the waves, and it took Dad a couple throws before I successfully caught the towline. I had reeled in a lot of fish, but it was much harder to reel in my dad and the *Little Minnow*. The wind and currents in the bay kept pulling him away from the boat.

After some time, we finally got the small boat close enough for Dad to connect to the *Orca II*. After tying down the lifeboat, Dad unzipped his backpack, pulling out the satellite tracking tag he had borrowed from Dr. Lott. At first, I was shocked. It didn't look like much and was quite a bit smaller than I had envisioned. I wasn't sure if this was something Dad should have risked his life for. The satellite tag was about five inches in length and had a small metal antenna coming out of the top.

"How does this electronic tag work?" I asked.

"This is a satellite tag. Whenever the tagged shark comes close to the top of the water or breaches, it transmits the location to a satellite receiver, which sends a loud ping to the laptop. This will help us know exactly where Monster is," Dad explained. "It works until the battery dies, then the tag falls off and floats. It sends a retrieval signal back to us so we can pick up the tag. And that's the good news."

"What's the bad news," I asked.

"There's only one way to tag a shark. We have to get close to Monster, real close. The tag has to be driven into the back of the shark, near the dorsal fin. We attach the tracking tag to the end of a pole and stab into the shark. Dr. Lott didn't have enough time to fully charge the tag. He said we should have at least four to five days before the battery goes dead."

Given it was Tuesday afternoon, that meant the tag probably wouldn't make it until Saturday night, the night of the mega-surfing event.

"It's our best and only option, son."

Getting the tag was challenging enough, but we weren't out of danger yet. We still had to find and tag the potentially biggest great white shark ever recorded. We had to do it without making a big scene and drawing any attention to the shark.

The ocean was vast, and Monster could be anywhere. But finding the shark wasn't going to be the hardest part. Getting within two feet of the mammoth-sized great white shark was going to be the greatest challenge.

-25-

It was late morning by the time we arrived near the last location we had seen the blue whale. Dad knew that sharks, especially large great whites, love to patrol and protect their food.

"Dad, what are the chances that Monster is still here?"

The location was almost at the halfway point between the Farallon Islands and our dock at Half Moon Bay. I remember learning in our science class that great white sharks can travel long distances. They migrate from their feeding grounds off the central California coast and can travel 2,500 miles away in the open ocean.

"What makes this situation so dangerous is

that Half Moon Bay is only about 15 miles away. We must make sure Monster heads back west towards Farallon and not to the east," said Dad as he reached into one of the onboard coolers and pulled out a bottle of water.

"Dad, there's a lot of ocean out here. Monster must have eaten quite a bit of the blue whale already," I said.

"He was probably pretty full for the past two days. This is as good as anywhere else to start, even though he may be hunting again. Monster might be tired of the elephant seals on Farallon and stayed around here."

Our hope was that there was still something left of the whale, and Monster had stayed close to protect his free meal.

I watched the GPS fish finder as it mapped our course. Dad had to use some math and calculate ocean currents to give us a general area of where the whale carcass could have floated. The machine showed the boat's path in a yellowish, orange line, giving us a grid perimeter to search for the whale. After finding the original spot where the *Atlantis* went down, Dad maneuvered our boat in a figure-eight pattern, searching for the carcass.

After an hour of seeing nothing, I started to get discouraged. The chances seemed slim to locate the whale carcass in the open ocean. Dad banked the boat and started heading west when I saw a huge flock of seagulls in the distance. Dad saw them too and turned the boat in their direction.

"I think we've found our whale," Dad said, knowing the birds were a sign of something dead in the water.

During our search, we had headed west, much closer to the California shoreline and home. I could see the coastline on the horizon, but that wasn't the only thing that caught my eye. There were boats in every direction.

For some reason, Dad stopped the boat. I was confused because we still had a long way to go to get to the crash site.

"Quick! Grab a pole and act like we're fishing," Dad said hurriedly.

I quickly grabbed the closest rod and held it up as though I were fishing on the bottom.

Boats started zooming past us, heading west, loaded with tourists excited to fish the Pacific Ocean. Most of the charter boats fished 5-10 miles offshore. Only the real adventure seekers were heading to the Farallon Islands to fish, whale watch, and hopefully catch a breaching great white.

At least twice as many boats were on the water than normal. One bright-yellow boat with red lettering caught my eye as it zoomed past us at a high rate of speed. It was going so fast I had trouble making out the name. I grabbed the binoculars just in time to make out *Froth* on the back of the boat.

It was Biggs' boat, and it was obvious they were going somewhere in a hurry. We both knew they weren't fishing; they were hunting.

-26-

The number of boats created quite a substantial wake even out in the open ocean. The noise from Biggs' boat belonged at a rock concert—not out on the Pacific.

The boats soon disappeared in the open water, and the morning rush to find Monster had soon sped past us. It took a couple minutes for the water to settle down, and then Dad pushed the boat's throttle, and we resumed heading toward the birds in the distance.

As we neared them, an object started to materialize—the whale carcass, or at least what was left of it. Besides having huge shark bite marks, it was obvious a lot of animals had taken advantage of the free meal. The carcass, which was only about ten feet in length now, showed no signs of the green slime; most of it must have been eaten or washed away.

Dad cut the engine and let the current take us over to the carcass.

"What now?" I asked.

"We wait," said Dad.

We floated near the decaying carcass for about an hour when we felt a nudge on the boat. There could only be one white shark big enough to move the *Orca II*.

Dad ran and opened up his backpack to retrieve the shark tag.

"Grab the pole!" Dad yelled.

I ran to the bow of the boat and pulled the long gaff that we used for larger sportfish. I handed the pole to Dad as he went to work, mounting the tracking beacon onto it.

"We only have one shot; we have to make it count," Dad said as a dorsal fin circled the boat and cut towards the whale carcass. Monster was showing her predatory behavior, trying to protect the whale carcass.

When the shark's dorsal fin breached the water, it confirmed what we already knew—it was Monster—there was no mistaking it. The shark's dorsal fin had two distinctive indentions in it.

Even though we knew it was Monster, the shark had grown even more. There was no doubt the shark was easily over 24 feet. It had grown an additional two feet! Bones was right, eating the blue whale that was saturated in nuclear waste caused the shark to grow at an alarming rate. Overall, Monster had grown four to five feet in three days. The effects of the nuclear waste were revealed and made Monster look unreal.

The shark circled our boat twice; it was obvious he didn't want us near the whale. The closer the shark got, the larger it loomed. It looked like the size of a school bus as it roared towards us. The shark turned as it neared the boat, giving Dad a small window to land the tag.

Dad pulled back and thrust the gaff with all his strength, landing it just below the shark's dorsal fin. Feeling the pressure of the thrust, Monster dove straight down towards deeper water away from the boat. As the huge dark shadow disappeared into the depths of the ocean, I could see a small, red blinking light.

Dad had hit his mark, and the tracking tag was activated!

"Did you see the size of that thing!" Dad shouted. I was still shaking and could barely answer.

Seeing a 24-foot great white shark swimming aggressively in the ocean was surreal. The size of the shark was going to make our problem even bigger.

"Dad, how are we supposed to keep Monster safe? A shark that big has nowhere to hide!"

"We just need to keep it away from Half Moon Bay and Pillar Point until that dumb surfing competition is over. By Saturday night, all the tourists will be on their way back home, and Biggs won't have to worry about a mega shark canceling his plans," Dad explained.

Dad stopped talking when his laptop let out a loud ping sound. We ran over, and Dad opened up his computer. There, glowing on the screen was a 3-D map with red dots on it.

"Whenever her dorsal comes near the top, the satellite tag will get a signal and send a loud ping to my computer," Dad said.

Monster's first ping showed the shark about a half mile west of our location. The good news was at least she was heading away from the shoreline, but the bad news was she was heading towards all the boats. The last thing Monster needed was to be the star of another viral video.

The great white just had to stay out of sight for four more days.

-27-

When we pulled back into the marina, it was a madhouse—a complete circus. People milled around everywhere, cell phones in hand, snapping pictures and boarding charter boats.

A loud buzzing sound caught my attention, and I peered to my left to see a bright, yellow helicopter scanning the shoreline.

"Just another one of Biggs' toys, no doubt," Dad said, shaking his head.

Biggs was going to pull out all the stops to ensure the surfing contest went on without a hitch or a big shark.

After tying down the *Orca II*, we took off down the docks, maneuvering our way through all the traffic as we headed toward the truck. Turning the corner to the parking lot, we were greeted by a blond man in a suit surrounded by people fawning over him.

"Lance Biggs," the man said, lifting his chin as if to see if we recognized him.

Dad gave him the "we-aren't-friends" look.

"Nice to meet you. I'm Corey James, and this is my son, Casey," said Dad.

"Groovy, nice to meet you, bruh. Listen, as you probably have heard or seen, this is a big weekend for me," Biggs said, pointing to a huge billboard behind him advertising the Mavericks FROTH Surfing competition.

Dad didn't really react, which kind of burned Biggs.

"Anyway, we're looking to book as many charter boats as possible the rest of the week. I'll pay you double what everyone else is paying," Biggs offered.

"What kind of fish are you interested in?" Dad asked.

"Fishing? Oh, no, my dear friend, we just want

to go whale watching or see some dolphins or something," explained Biggs.

"Sorry, but I'm booked the rest of the week. We can't help," said Dad as he pulled my arm to walk away.

It was obvious Biggs wasn't used to being told no. He smiled and moved out of our way so we could get to our truck. Just as we were about to leave, the laptop in Dad's backpack pinged. *Monster must have surfaced, and the alert couldn't have come at a worst time.*

"Wait!" Biggs ordered. "What was that?"

There wasn't much time to think, and Dad was a thinker; he rarely spoke without thinking.

"Hey, Corey, don't worry about the text you just got. It was just me. Catch any fish?" a voice from behind all the men asked.

Everyone turned, and there leaning against the wall, wearing his worn, blue, old Navy hat was Bones.

He joined us as Dad and I continued towards the truck. When we got there, I turned back towards Biggs and his henchman and saw they were still standing there and staring at us. They had a suspicion something wasn't quite right.

"Don't worry about them; we got bigger problems," said Bones.

Bigger problems than a multimillionaire trying to track down and kill the biggest great white shark ever on record?

"The A.E.C. called in a team; they're getting their gear together to go look for Monster," shared Bones. "They're planning on spending the next three days scouring the Farallon Islands looking for Monster."

Ping! Another loud noise erupted from Dad's laptop.

"They can go to the Farallon Islands all they want; Monster isn't there," Dad said, flipping open his computer screen.

The three of us just stared. Monster was pinging, but it wasn't near the Farallon Islands. The shark was much farther east than anyone thought and only five miles from Pillar Point.

-28-

"That should buy us some time. I told the A.E.C. that we were much closer to the Farallon Islands, so that's where they plan on starting," said Bones.

I stopped the old man.

"What's that in your hand? What are you drinking?" I asked.

Bones held up a bright-yellow can with FROTH outlined in red. I knew right away what it was; I had seen those stupid colors all week.

I walked over and grabbed the energy drink can from his hand, found a nearby garbage can, and threw it away. Bones just stood there staring at me.

"Why did you do that?" he asked, scratching his head. "It was actually pretty good."

"Those are garbage and will kill you. Every time you buy one, it just gives Mr. Biggs more money to hunt Monster," I said.

"There are coolers everywhere, plus it was free," protested Bones.

I looked out over the bay and sighed loudly. I couldn't believe how many boats had invaded Half Moon Bay. Everywhere you looked was a picture of Lance Biggs or some yellow-and-red sign advertising FROTH.

"We need a plan," said Bones.

"We have a plan," Dad quickly responded.

"That tag was a good idea, but we still need a plan," said Bones.

Right then a huge black truck pulled into the marina. In the distance, a high-dollar black boat was floating up to the boat ramp to be picked up. The boat was like something out of a sci-fi novel. Gadgets and gizmos were fixed all over it.

"They're here," Bones whispered, trying not to show interest.

"They've been here. They left right after us this morning," Dad said.

The Atomic Energy Commission had arrived just in time to get into the craziness of looking for Monster. The problem was they needed to do research on the shark to cover up their nuclear waste spill. In order to do that, they were going to kill Monster and take the carcass to one of their lab facilities.

"They're afraid some of that waste was digested through the blue whale into the shark. That would be horrible news for the commission and will mean a lot of big money lawsuits from animal rights organizations," said Bones. "They won't let that happen. They'll do anything to stop it. They can't let a 22-foot shark filled with their radioactive waste kill someone during Mavericks."

"Well, the good news is they won't find a 22-foot shark. The shark is now well over 24 feet," Dad told him.

Bones fell back against the truck in disbelief. "That's unheard of!"

"So is dumping radioactive waste in the Pacific Ocean," responded Dad with a sigh.

-29-

That night Dad let me keep the laptop computer in my room. I woke up three times to Monster's
pinging, telling me the shark was cruising between
five and ten miles offshore. I wondered if the shark
ever rested. *Did it know that it was being hunted?*

The early morning sun woke me up before the
alarm on my cell phone. Dad had already left for
his morning fishing charter, and Mom and Sara
were eating breakfast. I really wanted to take the
laptop to school. I didn't want to go all day not
knowing if Monster were safe.

But I knew there was no way I could take something so valuable to middle school. Dad spent more
money on that laptop than most people spend on a

car. It was loaded with special maps and fishing locations, making it even more valuable to Dad and the *Orca II*. Plus, I didn't want those stupid seventh graders to know anything about the tag or what I knew about the giant shark. I checked it before heading out the door, but no new pings.

The school week had been chaotic. Kids were giddy all week; the atmosphere felt more like we were getting ready for Christmas or Spring Break. Too bad that it was only early November. This was all because of a giant shark and the Mavericks FROTH Surfing Championship!

Kids spent most of the day either talking about it or showing pictures to each other on their cellphones. It appears Lance Biggs was very active in the Half Moon Bay area that week. Kids thought they were super cool because they either had taken a picture with Biggs or had random shots of him holding a FROTH.

I was really starting to hate those energy drinks even more. For one, kids shouldn't be drinking them; they weren't safe. A FROTH was filled with 60 grams of sugar and a boatload of caffeine. Even knowing that, kids were drinking them by record numbers. FROTH sales were up across the country. In Southern California alone, there was a 500-percent increase from October.

Every wannabe surfer or trendy social media video seemed to sport the bright yellow-and-red FROTH colors. Biggs looked like a marketing genius. His grand prize purse of $500,000 garnered a lot of national attention for both the Mavericks and for FROTH.

Monster's viral video just added to the circus and had been seen by over 10 million people on various social media sites. The original file was translated into 10 different languages and had views from over 40 countries.

After lunch, the day went from a slow crawl to a virtual halt. Seconds felt like weeks, and I had to play mind games to stop myself from looking at the clock. I stared at the whiteboard, wondering if Monster were still alive and safe. The thought of someone killing it, or tearing and dissecting it was making me sick to my stomach. I knew Dad's charter fishing trip was near San Francisco Bay. They were trolling for salmon and halibut. The chances of him seeing or hearing anything about Monster were very small.

Finally, the 3:00 dismissal bell rang, and my misery finally ended. I ran out of school and straight toward our house. I made it home in record time, completely out of breath.

I flipped open the laptop. No new pings from the satellite tag. The last recorded mark was at 4:00 this morning.

Did Biggs find her? Did the big fancy, A.E.C. boat rush Monster away in the dark to their secret lab? For the next two hours I sat staring at the green-colored screen, hoping and praying for Monster to ping.

My trance-like state was interrupted when Dad walked into the room.

"Any pings?" Dad asked.

"Nothing since this morning," I said with a worried expression.

"Remember the tag only alerts when Monster's dorsal fin comes close to the top or breaches the water. Maybe the shark is full or just hanging low today," Dad said. "There was a lot of chatter on the boat radio; a lot of people are out looking for the shark. I think I would have heard something from someone if they had spotted Monster."

Dad is probably right. If Monster had been seen or caught, it would be all over the news and social media.

That night for supper we ate fresh butter-roasted halibut with asparagus and olives because of Dad's successful charter trip. They had caught a lot of fish, and he was able to bring some home for dinner.

After dinner, our family sat down in the basement. Dad was watching WPIV Channel 6 for the local news and weather. I started watching it, hoping for no new shark videos. Thankfully, there was nothing about Monster; the entire news was dedicated to the Mavericks and Lance Biggs.

Yuck! I zoned out and decided to play an online game on my phone instead.

A couple minutes later I heard Dad's voice.

"Well, that's good news, Casey," said Dad.

"Oh, yeah, cool," I said not even looking up. I

was too engrossed in my game to hear what was on television.

"Casey, look!" Dad said pointing at the weather forecast. The weather for tomorrow had a 100-percent chance of rain and storms all day combined with a high wind advisory.

"No boats will be going out tomorrow," declared Dad.

I fell asleep to the sound of some documentary Dad was watching on the Industrial Revolution. The narrator had a dull voice that made it easy to fall into a deep sleep.

A loud noise broke my slumber. I rolled over, realizing Dad must have helped me to bed. I reached over and grabbed my cell phone, 3:32 a.m. I rolled over, closing my eyes which were still heavy from the lack of good sleep. The noise beeped again, jolting me out of bed and toward the laptop.

It wasn't Monster. It was just a stupid popup ad for the Mavericks FROTH Surfing Championship.

-30-

The hammering of the outside shutters slamming woke me up ten minutes before my alarm was to go off. The weatherman was right; the weather was awful. Rain was pounding on the roof, and high winds were shaking the trees. *Perfect weather to stay inside and leave Monster alone*, I thought. I figured the countdown was on. After today we would have less than 48 hours until the Mavericks tournament.

As long as Monster was safe, Lance Biggs could smile at the cameras and get all the publicity he wanted.

Once that happened, Bones had promised us to go to the local news station and tell the story, exposing the illegal dumping and the A.E.C's involvement.

Either most of the students were coming down from the sugar rush of drinking so many FROTH energy drinks or the dark, dreary Wednesday weather depressed them.

Either way, it didn't matter to me. I was just glad I didn't have to see any more pictures or hear kids bragging about Lance Biggs. It was a typical, boring Wednesday at school. I thought it was a perfect day until the loudspeaker came on right before our final dismissal bell. The sound crackled as Principal Jones' voice echoed through the old speakers.

"Casey James, please come to the principal's office immediately!"

That was it, short and sweet. I grabbed my stuff and threw it in my backpack. Walking out of class I could hear other kids snickering and laughing; I was so embarrassed. Halfway down the hall, it hit me—I was in trouble for throwing the kid's cell phone in the garbage. I knew it was coming and was surprised it took two days to get the call from the office.

I strolled in to the office and sat down. They had little red chairs for the kids who were short. I couldn't see Mrs. Parker, the secretary, but I could hear her typing. She picked up her phone and started having a conversation with someone.

"You can go in now, dear," said Mrs. Parker's raspy voice.

I got up and walked through the main office and opened Mr. Jones' door. He had etched glass on his door, so I wasn't sure if he was in there or not.

As the door slowly opened, I could see two men sitting at his table. One was Mr. Jones; the other was Lance Biggs. I was shocked at first and paused when I entered.

"It's okay, Casey, come on in," said Mr. Jones.

Lance was decked out in a full pin-striped yellow-and-red suit. Those colors were starting to repulse me, but they really brought out the blue in Biggs' eyes. Lance had the typical California surfer look—a great tan and blond, flowing hair.

Mr. Jones stood up, proud as a peacock, chest puffed up. "This is Lance Biggs," he said.

I smiled and acted impressed. For a second,

Biggs, who didn't get up to greet me, looked at me with a strange look. The look quickly vanished and was replaced with a silky, fake smile. *Biggs would make a perfect politician,* I thought.

"Hey, kid," he said, tossing me a bright-yellow FROTH shirt.

"Umm…thanks," I managed to say before being cut off by Mr. Jones. I could tell I wasn't there over the incident in the cafeteria with the cell phone.

"We'll make this short, Casey, since I am sure you're ready to get home. Mr. Biggs was kind enough to donate $15,000 to our school today towards the new science lab."

With a confused look, I scanned both men, hoping to get some type of hint as to why they wanted to talk to me. The thought of Biggs donating money for a science lab while trying to kill Monster angered me even more.

Without breaking stride, Mr. Jones continued, "Mr. Biggs here was hoping you could help him on a small matter."

Biggs leaned in. "Let me get right to the point. Where's the shark, kid?" he asked in an evil tone.

I froze and didn't know what to say. I sat staring at both men, hoping they would just let me alone and let me leave. After a couple seconds, it was obvious that wasn't going to happen.

"Come on, son, Lance just wants to make sure nothing bad happens at the Mavericks this weekend," said Mr. Jones.

By something bad, did he mean killing an innocent shark? I knew what he was really saying. Lance wanted assurance that his million-dollar event was without shark sightings.

"Listen, kid, I also speak Española. I talked to those crew guys you saved. They told me the boat that saved them was the *Orca II*," Biggs declared.

There was actually a sigh of relief inside when he told me that. At first I thought Bones might have sold us out for a couple cases of FROTH since the old bird had trouble keeping his mouth shut. That also meant that Biggs didn't know about the shark tag either.

"Oh, yeah, that shark. We saw him near Farallon," I said. I technically wasn't lying; we were kind of near the islands if you consider ten miles close.

"Listen, kid, I already know that. Where exactly was the shark?" he demanded.

I did know where; in fact, I had the exact coordinates memorized. I figured Mr. Jones would know if I lied, plus at this point it didn't really matter. I knew Monster hadn't been back to that area in the past three days, having already eaten the rest of the blue whale carcass. "37°37′N 123°17′W," I said.

Biggs reached into his back pocket and unraveled some type of nautical map. I peeked over the edge and could see grid markings and what looked like tides and currents.

It was obvious Biggs' crew had been busy that week. The map had four or five different locations marked on the map. He was trying to determine where the shark's home range was and how far from the Farallon Islands the shark would travel to ensure that a swim to Half Moon Bay was out of the question.

Our mark was the farthest, meaning Monster had moved closer and closer to the coast all week. The last mark on Biggs' map was only ten miles off the coast.

Monster had been on the move, and, by all calculations, was closer than ever to the shoreline. An estimated 8,000 people would be boating or in the water for the upcoming Mavericks event.

"I have to find that shark," Lance said angrily as he walked towards Mr. Jones' door.

"Good luck, you have some major competition," I said.

He stopped and spun. "I will find this shark first—before anyone else!" he shouted.

"I'm just saying, rumor is that there's an even bigger player than you out there looking for the shark," I said.

"What? Trust me, no one has the resources that I have; there is no else like Lance Biggs," he declared.

"Might not be another Lance Biggs, but there is someone with a lot of cash looking for the great white. He's driving a brand-new, black 434 Super Cab Premier. Big money player. I saw the boat myself at the marina," I said.

I knew I had his attention.

The A.E.C.'s custom boat cost close to a million

dollars and was very recognizable when compared to the other boats at the Half Moon Bay Marina. I figured a little competition could draw Lance's attention away from the *Orca II* and Monster.

Lance smirked as he walked out of Mr. Jones' office. "Well, then, may the best man win."

-31-

I knew Lance Biggs couldn't let anyone show him up. So I figured it would be to our advantage to have him worry about the A.E.C.'s boat. It was still raining hard when I walked home. Knowing that Lance was aware that I had seen the shark was almost a relief. I tried to convince myself that Biggs would leave us alone because he would think he had squeezed me for all the information I had.

The rain continued throughout the night and all day Thursday. The computer was silent—not a single ping from Monster. I stayed away from Mr. Jones all day. I did whatever I could to avoid people and attention.

We didn't have school on Friday, which now

seemed a little fishy, but what eighth grader didn't like having a Friday off? I planned on joining Dad on one of his charter fishing trips. Two weeks earlier, Mr. Jones had sent a letter home, saying we would have the day off because the teachers had some special training. Everyone knew the letter was a cover-up for the Mavericks.

I kept trying to figure out how the long weekend would go. Mom greeted me at the front door with a towel. Two straight days of rain were starting to get tiresome.

"Honey, can you turn off the notifications on the computer in your room? That thing has been beeping all day," said Mom.

"Thanks for the towel," I said, sprinting to my room. *Ping! Ping!*

There were four new satellite alerts from Monster. After I got changed out of my wet clothes, I sat down at my desk looking at the different locations on the map. All of the pings were close to the Farallon Islands. It appeared Monster was on the hunt once again. The pings probably meant the shark was feeding. I figured he returned to fatten up on a seal after enjoying all the whale meat from earlier in the week. The alerts reaffirmed that Monster was alive and well. It also proved the shark and the weather were outsmarting the A.E.C. and Biggs.

Dad heard the beeping and came in. He smiled as he examined the locations on the computer.

"She's still going strong," he said with a grin.

The shark tag had become our biggest tool in the quest to protect Monster. The thirty-mile span to the Farallon Islands was deep and mysterious, making the hunt for Monster even harder for everyone else. The odds were in our favor, and hopefully, the giant shark could lay low until the Mavericks was over.

"Can you help me with a charter tomorrow?" Dad asked.

"I thought you'd never ask! I would love to! Where are we fishing?" I asked.

"How about the Farallon Islands?" Dad asked with a smile.

It was almost too good to be true. We knew Monster was at the islands, and as long as she stayed there and far away from the Mavericks, she would be safe. I really wanted to see the shark again. The weather forecast for the next three days was perfect. Dad had booked a charter that wanted to catch lingcod. The plan was to return to a couple of our favorite spots just south of Seal Rock outside of South Farallon Island.

"How many people are going on the charter?" I asked Dad.

"That's the weird thing. Originally it was supposed to be five. The Mavericks' surfing judges booked months ago. For some reason, they canceled last night. Within five minutes, someone booked an all-day charter online for one person. Plus, they paid a $500 bonus on top of the charter fee," said Dad, scratching his head.

"Who's name was on the booking?" I asked.

"There was no name left, just the initials F. E. on the payment," answered Dad.

-32-

The computer remained silent all night Thursday. Sleep had come at a premium that week, but not Thursday night. I slept soundly through the entire night.

The fishing report for Friday morning was excellent. After we had gotten hammered with bad weather for two days, the next three days were going to be gorgeous ones. The forecast called for lots of sun and very little wind.

Dad and I arrived at the docks around 5:15 a.m. It was ironic how I could jump out of bed before my alarm clock to go fishing. When it came time to get up for school, Mom practically had to drag me out of bed.

The weekend was finally here, and the docks were full of excitement. As soon as we arrived at the boat, I started going through my specific first-mate jobs. I always began with checking the poles and making sure there was plenty of fishing line on the reels. Once that was done, my next job was checking on the bait in the live well to make sure we had plenty of squid. Then I made sure all the lines were connected and aerating the water so the bait stayed fresh.

I was working at the live well when I heard Dad talking to someone. I glanced over and watched as a taller, slender man stepped on board the *Orca II*.

"Casey, come on up here," Dad hollered from the cabin of the boat. I shut the live well hatch and started towards the cabin.

Our client was in the cab with his back to me looking out the window. He turned towards me as I walked in.

"Hello, Casey," said the man.

It was Lance Biggs.

F.E. was none other than Biggs himself. I just stared at him, then it hit me—FROTH ENERGY.

"We meet again, kid. It seems like our paths keep intersecting," he said. We both knew why Biggs was there. Dad had already taken payment for the charter and lived by a code of ethics when it came to charter fishing. Since Biggs had paid, it was the job of Saltwater Fishing Adventures to take him fishing.

"I think you guys know where I want to go to first, but let's make a little stop on our way to the island," he said. He wanted to visit the *Atlantis* crash site—the original spot where Monster had been filmed. He pulled out his map—the same map I had seen at school. The map looked a little different as it had several new markings outlined on it. Lance hadn't wasted any time or money on finding Monster. He had multiple crews out around the clock, trying to find the shark.

"Biggs, remember we're a fishing charter boat," Dad said sternly.

"Of course, I enjoy fishing and was told the *Orca II* finds the fish and that they seem to always be in the right spot," he said.

We knew he was referring to Monster. He had

paid off the judges so he could be on the *Orca II* with Dad and me. This was his last hope. Things were coming down to the wire, and he was living in constant fear of having to cancel the Mavericks FROTH event.

Awkwardness filled the boat as we traveled to the spot of the sinking cargo ship. The three of us sat in the cabin, and no one talked. Biggs just sat on the stool, sipping on a FROTH. The water was calm, reflecting the bright sunlight and making it look like blue glass.

Biggs was on his cell phone for most of the ride to the site. When we arrived at the exact location, Biggs looked around for a couple minutes. Seeming satisfied, he walked back into the cabin.

"I don't know what you're looking for, but there's nothing here," said Dad.

"I'm just making sure I don't leave any stones unturned. That's all, Corey," said Biggs. "Feel free to head towards the Farallon Islands."

The boat veered and roared straight east towards the Island of the Dead. After a couple minutes of complete silence, Biggs finally spoke.

"So, kid, you like surfing? I could score you some sweet V.I.P. tickets for the competition tomorrow," he offered.

"I like fishing" was all I could manage to say.

He nodded and went back to texting on his cell phone. During the ride I tried to think of things to get my mind off the monster that was riding in our cabin. Nothing worked—not even the thought of fishing adventures.

Just when I thought I was going to go crazy, the outline of the Farallon Islands appeared on the horizon.

Every time I saw them, it was amazing. The view and the feeling never got old. Biggs even showed a smile of admiration when he saw the islands.

But his moment of awe only lasted a minute or so. "What is that smell? It's disgusting!" he said, making a gagging noise.

The *Orca II* motored towards one of our favorite fishing spots just off Seal Rock, about a half mile from the South Farallon Island. The location was right above a rocky shelf that separated the shallow and deep water, a perfect spot for fishing.

After grabbing a handful of fresh squid, I baited six lines and dropped them to the bottom. Within an hour, we already had five fish in the boat, but there were no great white sightings.

The fishing didn't seem to be exciting enough for Lance. It was obvious he was getting bored with catching lingcod. There were several other boats fishing the islands and one boat that was on a shark and whale watching tour.

There were a number of new boats that I had never seen at Farallon before. I grabbed the binoculars and noticed some weren't fishing; it was clear they were hunting.

While scanning the field of boats, one in particular caught my eye. It was bright-yellow and stood out like a sore thumb.

"You have some of your guys out here?" I asked disgusted.

"The more eyes the better," said Biggs.

Biggs had arranged for his personal boat, the *Froth*, to follow us out to Farallon. I knew that wasn't the only boat that he had invited out on the water with us.

At a low speed, the *Froth* was crisscrossing the area, making a strange pattern. I squinted and could make out two men at the back of the boat with buckets. *They aren't fishing, so what are they up to?*

As we got closer, I could see the men dumping the buckets overboard. They were chumming. Chumming is used to attract sharks by dumping fish blood and bones into the water. The blood in the water attracts sharks, and they began to come to the surface to feed on the pieces of fish.

"Lance, you know that's illegal!" I said as I turned toward him.

"Accidently spilling bait is illegal? Besides it's only illegal if you get caught," he replied.

"Why did you charter our boat when you could have just come out on your own boat?" Dad demanded.

"You know so much more about the giant shark than you're letting on. I'm not letting that beast anywhere near Pillar Point. That shark isn't going to ruin my surfing competition," he said, pounding his fist on the table.

"You're the only real monster out here, Biggs," Dad declared, glaring at him.

Just then a group of seals crested swimming near the boat. The seals splashed and swam frantically for the safety of Seal Rock. In the deep water, the seals are vulnerable to an attack from great whites. The playfulness of the seals changed as they dove beneath the water. Lurking behind them, a large dark shadow was on the hunt.

The three of us moved to the bow of the boat and watched as a shark swam just feet away from the *Orca II*. We stood motionless as it went under the boat. The sheer size of the shark took Lance by surprise as he fumbled to pull out a cell phone.

It was Monster! Lance had seen with his own eyes the massiveness of the 24-foot great white shark. He held the phone to his ear, "Guys, the shark is between us. Quick! Head our way. Be prepared to take it out."

In the distance, the *Froth* turned and roared towards us. The bright-yellow boat left a huge chum line as it scooted our way.

-33-

I had hoped the sound of the boat would push Monster down into deeper water, but it didn't. This shark was the apex predator in the Pacific Ocean. She feared nothing. The *Froth* pulled within 100 yards of our boat. The cloud of chum had followed them right towards us.

Everyone lost sight of Monster as the *Froth* idled. Lance was on the phone frantically instructing his men. I noticed one of the men went into the cabin and returned with a huge gaff hook. The other man followed, holding a powerhead.

A powerhead, also known as a Boomstick, is a specialized firearms weapon that can be shot under water. They are usually used for spear fishing and can fire a large projectile that can kill a shark. But the shark had to be in close range, and it only had one shot before reloading. This Boomstick seemed much bigger than any I had ever seen. Biggs was there for one reason—to kill Monster. They had baited the giant shark by filling the ocean with chum. It was just a matter of time before she surfaced again.

"Lance, what are you doing?" Dad asked.

Biggs, still on his cell phone, turned in Dad's direction, then quickly turned back to watch his boat.

In the distance, to the east of the *Froth*, a huge dorsal fin appeared out of the chum-filled water. The fin indention was obvious; Monster was heading directly towards the *Froth*. The men maneuvered to the front of the boat and closed the distance to the shark.

Ping!

Biggs turned towards the cabin as he hung up his cell phone.

"What was that?" he yelled.

"Just my Fish-finder marking fish. You better not kill that shark!" Dad yelled.

"That shark isn't getting any closer to the Mavericks," Biggs shouted back.

After taking several aggressive steps towards Lance, Dad turned and jogged back into the cabin and hit the throttle on the boat.

The *Orca II* took off so fast Lance and I had to grab the side of the boat to keep from falling down. Dad took aim at the front of the *Froth*.

"What are you doing, dude? Are you crazy?" Biggs yelled, trying to crawl towards the cabin. The speed and commotion of the *Orca II* pushed Monster down again before the crew on the *Froth* had a chance at Monster. Dad pulled back the throttle with about ten feet to go before ramming the boat. It was a move that can only be done by an expert. Anyone else would have slammed directly into the side of the *Froth*.

Biggs crew stood on the deck, visibly shaken. They were petrified of becoming shark bait.

Dad walked over and grabbed Lance by the back of his neck, picking him up off the deck. My dad was a big man, much bigger than Lance. In all my years, I never saw my dad lose his temper until now. There was a crazed look in his eyes that even had me shaking. He took Biggs over to the edge of the boat and dangled him over the open water.

Biggs was just barely a foot above the bloody chum-filled water. At any second, Biggs knew he could be Monster's next meal.

Lance was pleading with my dad to bring him back into the boat. His men were yelling; the whole scene was pure chaos.

"You will never step foot in my boat again," Dad shouted.

The *Froth* moved much closer to the *Orca II* and threw over a safety line. I caught it and started pulling their boat closer to us. I knew Dad was strong, but he couldn't hold Biggs much longer.

When the *Froth* got within a couple feet of our boat, Dad took both hands and threw Lance onto their deck.

Biggs landed with a loud thud but was safe.

"Get out of here before I call the shore patrol," Dad threatened.

Biggs tried to stand up but fell right back down. Dad shot a salty glare across to Lance as he retreated into the cabin. Seconds later, the engine roared on the *Froth*, and the boat sped away.

"Dad, you could have killed him," I said as I watched the *Froth* speed off.

"How? He could have swam to his boat," Dad replied.

"But the sharks—he wouldn't have lasted a second in these waters," I said.

"No, they would have spit him right back out. Sharks don't like the taste of rats," Dad said with a smile.

-34-

I was filled with pride for the moment. Dad had saved Monster and put a rich, spoiled bully in his place.

Some of the other boats had seen the commotion and radioed my dad. He played it off like it wasn't a big deal—just a simple misunderstanding.

"Monster is safe for now. Lance is too scared and embarrassed to stay out here any longer. I don't think he enjoyed his first trip to the Farallon Islands as much as we did," Dad said to me with another smile.

Dad started the engine and headed back to Half Moon Bay Harbor. Time was crucial, so Dad opened up the throttle as high as it would go. A couple miles before Old Moon Bay, I noticed a big boat heading toward us.

At first I thought Lance had found some courage and was coming back to finish off Monster. But the boat wasn't yellow; it was black. As it motored past us, it was clearly the A.E.C., and their route was directly towards the islands.

"Can't worry about that now; we have to get back to Half Moon Bay," Dad said.

As we pulled into the harbor, most of the slips were empty. The boats were out on the ocean and still had a couple of hours of good fishing. Looking past the docks, I spotted the bright-yellow *Froth* still sitting in its boat slip. Dad had hoped we could beat them back to the docks to control the story, but our boat couldn't keep up with the speedy *Froth*. They had beaten us back.

It looked like the boat was empty. I quickly tied up the *Orca II* and grabbed my backpack. Dad was already halfway down the dock, and I had to jog to catch up to him.

At the end of the dock, we saw that another crowd had assembled. I saw there were multiple television cameras and news reporters crowded around Lance Biggs.

"Fans have nothing to worry about. There are no big sharks close to Point Pillar or the Mavericks. I just got back from a trip and can happily say there are no great white sharks around. Our safety team has already prepped the area for tomorrow. The Mavericks Championship is happening," Biggs declared.

The guy was smooth. As soon as his feet had hit dry land, his ego had turned him back into the billionaire surfer.

We stood in the back listening to Lance brag about his celebrity friends who would be attending the Mavericks event. The reporters fell for his charm, and he had them all eating out of his hand.

Knowing this was going nowhere, Dad intervened. "Lance, did you tell them about the environmental issue your guys found?" yelled Dad.

The television cameras whirled on Dad and me as we stood there on the edge of the dock. Lance looked as confused as I did. I couldn't help but wonder what in the world Dad was doing.

"That's right, Lance and his team uncovered some potential hazard nuclear waste just outside the Farallon Islands. It's some very dangerous stuff. In fact, he devoted all his companies' resources and finances to the clean-up process," said Dad.

The cameras quickly panned back to Lance.

"Yes, that's right," Lance quickly replied.

Reporters started yelling out questions and asking what kind of waste was found and who put it there.

"In fact, Sergeant James Mitchell, a former engineer at the Atomic Energy Commission, will fill you all in," said Dad.

Bones stepped out of the shadow, and his gray, wrinkled face was illuminated in the camera light. He stared straight into the reporters' eyes and started to tell his story about the *U.S.S. Independence* and his work with the A.E.C.

We slipped out of the back of the crowd and headed to the parking lot.

"Dad, why did you do that? The A.E.C. is going to go after Bones for exposing them," I said.

"I had no choice. Bones and I had talked about

it at great length. He is the one who suggested it this way, I think it was his way of making up for his mistake," said Dad.

Dad added, "It's the only way to save face with Biggs and stop the A.E.C. from killing Monster."

We stayed and watched for the next ten minutes as Bones shared with the crowd his nuclear waste-dumping story.

"I think we can head home now," Dad said.

We left Bones to be the celebrity and headed toward the parking lot. After climbing in the passenger side of the truck, I heard a loud, strange noise coming from behind the restaurant. The noise started getting louder and louder. We jumped out of the truck in time to see Lance's yellow helicopter elevate straight in the air, then turn, heading east toward the Farallon Islands.

-35-

Bones' interview was all over the local news and started an immediate investigation into the Atomic Energy Commission's involvement in the nuclear waste dumping. Within 30 minutes of the interview, locals reported seeing a huge black boat return to Old Moon Bay harbor. Three men quickly loaded the boat on a trailer and disappeared. There was no doubt that we didn't have to worry about the A.E.C. hurting Monster anymore.

During the interview, Bones didn't mention anything about the shark or the effects the radiation had on her body. The shark had grown four feet in the past three days due to her exposure to the radioactive waste.

One predator down—the A.E.C.—and after tomorrow's Mavericks event, Biggs would leave Monster alone. The shark just had to stay around the Farallon Islands, far away from the coastline and from the Mavericks.

When we got home, I plugged in the laptop and put it on my desk. It took Dad a couple hours to calm down.

That evening people around Half Moon Bay and Pillar Point were out enjoying local restaurants and having fun. Surfers competing in the Mavericks FROTH Surfing Championship were full of anticipation, hoping to ride the gigantic Mavericks the next day. Some dreamed of the $500,000 prize money while others were content on just having a chance to board the Mavericks.

There was a sense of happiness all around, and most were enjoying the start to a star-studded weekend. But one small group of people who were aware of the real danger lurking closer and closer to Half Moon Bay and Pillar Point were restless and worried.

Dad and I planned to join hundreds of other

boats to watch the competition just outside of Half Moon Bay the next day. It allowed us to get a water view of the surfers but not get too close the dangerous waves of the Mavericks. It's a pretty cool scene with so many boats anchored watching the event. Mom and Sara planned on driving into San Francisco to spend the day shopping.

Saturday morning, I woke up with a sense of relief. I knew that we had done everything we could to help save Monster. I knew that no matter what happened, I wouldn't have to see FROTH cans littering my beautiful beach.

I was just ready to be done. I couldn't wait for it all to disappear, so Half Moon Bay could turn back into paradise. The idea of fishing in peace and quiet was something I had missed all week.

I woke up to the strong smell of chocolate chip pancakes and bacon. Dad wasn't much of a cook, but he enjoyed making us breakfast when he had the time.

The actual professional surfing competition was slated to start at 5:00 p.m. Biggs had planned a bunch of other entertaining gimmicks and had amateurs surfing the smaller side of Mavericks starting at 1:00 p.m.

We were in no rush and planned on leaving the house around noon. After breakfast, I took a shower and got dressed. I went to my room to grab the laptop computer to take with us just to make sure Monster stayed away. The computer had been quiet all night, so I walked over to close the top so it would fit better in my backpack. When I touched the lid, the computer came out of sleep mode to reveal the map.

I noticed several new locations were showing on the map. The strange thing was I hadn't heard a beep all night. But for some reason there were numerous new pings plotted out on the screen.

After examining the keyboard on the computer, I quickly found the issue. Somehow, in all the excitement on the boat yesterday, the mute button had accidentally gotten pushed.

Monster was active again and this time not near the Farallon Islands.

She had started pinging at 3:00 a.m. about twenty miles off the shoreline. Her next two alerts were at 5:00 a.m. and 7:00 a.m., showing the shark on a continuous track.

The great white was heading west, cruising at a much higher speed than usual.

The last ping was at 11:00 a.m. while I was in the shower. The alert showed the shark's location was eight miles due east of Pillar Point shore.

I threw the computer in my backpack and took off for the front door.

"Dad, we have to go; we have a big problem!" I said, grabbing one last pancake for the road.

We raced towards the harbor in Dad's truck. It took a lot longer to get back to Half Moon Bay than it normally did. Cars and people were everywhere. We tried pulling into the parking lot, but it was already full and closed.

We had to park a mile away and jog the rest of the way to the *Orca II*. Once we hit the dock, I noticed someone standing down by our boat. As we got closer, I could see Bones holding a black over-sized duffle bag.

"About time you boys got here," he said.

Bones and Dad started talking as I untied the

boat and got it ready to launch. Our boat was one of the only ones still in its slip.

Within minutes the boat was off and roaring towards Pillar Point. The Maverick's observation point was only a couple miles north of Old Moon Bay so it didn't take us long to get there.

As we pulled up, I was shocked at the number of people there. The calm cove water was filled with hundreds of boats and jet skis. People were tubing and water skiing, and kids were swimming in the open water. There was a high level of noise and commotion in the water.

"Looks like we have company," Dad said, pointing behind us. I turned to see the *Froth* idling a couple yards behind us. Three of Biggs goons were on board.

Strange…his boat didn't come from Old Moon Bay. How did it find us so fast? I thought. *How did they know we were here?*

Near the front of all the boats were the big money players—the Yacht Club as Dad called them. At the very front of the boats sat a massive yacht with the initials F. E. on the back. We knew Biggs was on it since he always had to be at the front and center of attention. I grabbed the binoculars and scanned the rest of the boats. There were several of his smaller boats had set up in an outside perimeter around the boats. The outside boats were prepared for any danger that might come to Biggs or the Mavericks.

Ping!

The three of us ran into the cabin. I pulled out the laptop, and the great white shark was only two miles southeast.

She was on a straight course heading towards the Mavericks!

-36-

"We have to lose Biggs' boat and get to Monster before the shark enters Pillar Point," Dad said, as he started the engine. There was no doubt in our mind the shark would come to investigate all the noise from the Mavericks.

If that happened, something very bad could happen. Monster was still a wild predator, and she was probably hungry.

Dad slowly maneuvered the boat, weaving around other boats, trying to lose the *Froth*. No matter where he went, the boat followed us closely. Biggs' boat seemed to know our every move. Hundreds of boats were surrounding the Mavericks, but Biggs' boat was able to stay right on our tail.

"We're running out of time. We have to keep that shark away from the Mavericks!" Dad said.

Our worry was not just for Monster, but now we had to worry about all the people in the water. Bones walked into the cabin and started opening all the drawers. He picked put up several cushions before reaching down and pulling an object out of the glove box. He walked out holding a cell phone.

"I think I know why the *Froth* is able to know exactly where we're going," said Bones.

Bones held up a smartphone. We were sure it belonged to Lance Biggs. During our trip to the Farallon Islands yesterday, he had left it to give him the perfect way to monitor the *Orca II*.

"Let's just throw it in the water. That will stop them," I said.

Bones walked over to the side of the boat and was just about to launch the cellphone into the Pacific when Dad yelled, "No, don't! Let's use Biggs' tracking trick to help save Monster. Bones, grab your bag."

Bones walked back into the cabin and returned with a black duffle bag. He unzipped and pulled out a strange-looking black object. The old man started to unfold and manipulate the object until it started to resemble a seal.

"We were going to drag that seal decoy behind the *Orca II* to lure Monster away from all these people and the Mavericks," Dad said. "We were going to lower him in the *Little Minnow* with the seal decoy. Then Bones and I were going to drive the *Orca II* north around the other side of the Mavericks. The *Froth* would follow, and hopefully Monster would follow the *Little Minnow* right out of Pillar Point Harbor.

"Let me do it," Bones pleaded. "Corey, this is something I need to do. Let me drive the *Little Minnow*."

Looking into Bones' eyes was all the convincing Dad needed. They told the story of a man seeking redemption, trying to right the wrongs he had made while working for the A.E.C.

-37-

Dad turned the *Orca II* sharply, making a figure-eight pattern around several boats. The aggressive move worked just enough to allow us to lower Bones in the *Little Minnow*.

Once in the water, the *Little Minnow* looked similar to many of the other smaller boats observing the Mavericks. Dad turned the *Orca II*, concealing Bones as he motored west away through the congested group of boats.

The *Froth* kept their distance and watched from a couple hundred yards away. Dad started the boat and drove slowly towards the front of the line of boats, towards Lance Biggs. He cut the engine as we drifted closer and closer to the yachts. We were within shouting distance of the yachts when Dad dropped the anchor.

I scanned the area with binoculars before turning west to check on Bones. In the distance, miles away, I could see the *Little Minnow* all by itself. The boat looked even smaller from this distance, but I could make a bouncing, black object skipping behind the boat.

All the other boats' attention and focus were to the east, towards the Mavericks. No one noticed the small boat break out from the pack.

After a couple minutes, I noticed someone staring at us from the deck of Biggs' yacht. I glanced through the binoculars to see a confused Lance Biggs glassing in our direction.

We smiled, waving towards Biggs.

He sat down his binoculars and went back to his party. The entire time the *Froth* idled just off our stern, waiting for us to make our next move. An hour went by as we sat enjoying the atmosphere of the Mavericks.

Ping!

We raced into the cabin. Monster pinged, but

this time it was a couple miles west. Bones had done it! He had managed to get Monster's attention and turn him away from the Mavericks. The seal decoy must have worked!

I slumped in my chair in relief and took a deep breath. "Let's head back to Old Moon Bay," I said to Dad.

"Don't you want to stick around see the Mavericks event?" Dad asked.

"No, I think I've had enough excitement this week. Let's go back and fish off the dock at Half Moon," I said.

The ignition rumbled on the *Orca II* as Dad turned the key. I pulled the anchor as we headed back towards Half Moon Bay.

The *Froth* quickly started their engine and followed behind us. They sat just off the end of the dock as we parked the *Orca II*. Biggs' men looked confused when we walked off the boat and started fishing off the dock.

It was 5:00 p.m. and the Mavericks FROTH Surfing Championship was about to start. Right on cue the *Froth* left, motoring back towards the

Mavericks. Their mission was done, and we were harmless. They knew we weren't going after Monster. Even if we were, it didn't matter now, the event was starting and Biggs was home free.

Monster didn't attack at Pillar Point and cancel the Mavericks event or harm any people.

Dad and I fished for about an hour. The laptop computer started to make a strange sound. It wasn't the normal ping alert sound—it was more audible and drawn-out.

"Battery on the tag died," Dad said.

Talk about perfect timing! The tag lasted long enough to save Monster. The computer showed the satellite tag about seven miles away, a safe distance away from the shore. It was clear that Bones was taking the shark back towards the Farallon Islands.

"Let's go pick up the satellite tag and grab Bones. I promised Dr. Lott that I would return it when we were done," Dad said.

We boarded the *Orca II* and headed out to grab Bones and the tag.

"Dad, how do you know Bones will be there?"

"He has to be in that general area. We only had

a half tank of gas in the *Little Minnow* so he can't be too much farther than that."

"But what about Monster?"

"She's long gone. I bet she's on her way back to the Farallon Islands. Plus, she wouldn't have enough time to make it to the Mavericks now anyway," said Dad.

We followed the GPS on the computer out into the open ocean. The satellite coordinates took us right to the small tracking tag. It was hard to see the tag in the waves and would have been impossible to find without the GPS. Dad reached down with the gaff and grabbed the tag.

"Strange, we should have seen Bones by now," Dad said.

We drove another three or four miles west before stopping the boat. Dad sat staring at the electronic onboard map.

"For some reason, these coordinates ring a bell," Dad said.

I looked at the map and knew right away.

"Dad, this is really close to the area where the *U.S.S. Independence* is buried," I said shocked.

I reached over and grabbed the small radio. "Bones, come in. Bones, where are you?" I shouted frantically.

There was no response—just radio silence.

Dad and I spent the rest of the night driving around the Pacific Ocean, looking for Bones and the *Little Minnow*. We found no sign of the old man or the boat. A search crew was sent out after we returned to Half Moon Bay. After three days and no sightings, the search was eventually called off.

A lot of ideas about Bones' disappearance ran through my mind. *Had the A.E.C. taken Bones to keep their secret? Did the small boat capsize in the big Pacific waves? Could this have been the perfect ending Bones was looking for?*

Bones wasn't the only one that had vanished that night in the sea. There were no more sightings of Monster—not at the Farallon Islands, or anywhere else.

And no one rode the left at the Mavericks.

About the Author

Lane Walker is an award-winning author, speaker and educator. His book collection, Hometown Hunters, won a Bronze Medal at the Moonbeam Awards for Best Kids Series.

In the fall of 2020, Lane launched another series called The Fishing Chronicles. Lane is an accomplished outdoor writer in the state of Michigan. He has been writing for the past 20 years and has over 250 articles professionally published.

Walker has a real passion for outdoor recruitment and getting kids excited about reading. He is a former 5th grade teacher and elementary school principal. Currently, he is a Director/Principal at a technical center in Michigan. Walker is married with four, amazing children. Find out more about the author at www.lanewalker.com

---